HARVEST
OF LOVE

HARVEST OF LOVE

•

MARSHA DRISCOLL

AVALON BOOKS
THOMAS BOUREGY AND COMPANY, INC.
401 LAFAYETTE STREET
NEW YORK, NEW YORK 10003

For Jean Adler, an extraordinary teacher whose love and dedication sustained a very special student.

Acknowledgments

Once again, I would like to thank Michael Bailey, wildlife biologist for the Hoover Nature Preserve and for Mudhen Marsh. He has been a patient teacher and a tireless worker for the urban wildlife areas in Columbus, Ohio. His explanations about the development and management of wetlands has been invaluable, especially when he provided the opportunity for me to freeze my wet toes while planting willow trees. If I've made any mistakes about the wildlife, it's my error, not his.

Prologue

Painfully, eleven-year-old Bitsy Traynor dragged the heavy maple branch across the dirt road. With each step the swelling in her right ankle increased, and she clenched her teeth to stop herself from crying. Even more distressing than the injury to her ankle was the twisted wreck of her bicycle, now lying at the side of the road. She thought about leaving things just as they were, picking up the remains of her bike, and limping back home, but a plaintive note whistled close to her feet, calling her back to her self-imposed task.

She knew she needed a more substantial barrier to prevent traffic from using this shortcut down to the reservoir. The old fire break saved a good ten minutes of biking time, and the local teenagers even drove their cars this way sometimes; if Bitsy's rescue work was to be successful, she would have to make it too much trouble for anyone to bother clearing the track. She

1

dropped the branch and headed back into the woods for another. Slowly the pile of rubble began to grow into an effective deterrent to traffic.

"Hey, kid! What are you doing?"

Bitsy was focused with single-minded determination on completing her job and did not even realize someone had approached. She was starting once more into the woods when she felt the strong hand grab her arm.

"I said, what are you doing?"

This time the voice penetrated her consciousness, and the pressure on her arm nearly caused her to lose her precarious balance. With a gasp of pain, she started to fall, but the strong hand held fast to her arm, and another hand reached out to support her around the waist.

"Hold on. Calm down."

Bitsy looked up into the serious, dark brown eyes of one of the many high school boys she had seen around her home. Josh Mason didn't recognize her, but she remembered him. He and at least a dozen other boys hovered around her four older sisters like ants around spilled sugar. Usually, Bitsy ignored the lot of them, but she had always noticed Josh. For one thing, he managed to keep his dignity around her sisters instead of always showing off with ridiculous stunts or fighting the other boys. For another thing, he talked about interesting things, like science and books, even though Bitsy knew he also played on the junior varsity basketball team. And best of all, he never made fun of Bitsy and her younger sisters. At least not until now.

"I said, are you all right?" Joshua's voice had taken on a tone of exasperation and he shook her just a little.

"I . . . I . . . I'm sorry," Bitsy finally managed to blurt out. "Yes. I'm all right. I just twisted my ankle a little."

Josh looked down at the injured joint and shook his head. All trace of irritation left his voice and he said sympathetically, "It looks more than just twisted. You've either sprained it or broken it." He reached down and curved his arm behind her knees, lifting her scrawny frame completely off the ground without even a grunt of exertion. Carrying her back to the main road, he placed her on the hood of his dirty blue pickup truck. Big blue eyes brimming with unspilled tears widened at this heroic feat.

"Let me take a look," he insisted, gently untying her sneaker and carefully pulling it off her foot. "What were you doing, anyway?"

Bitsy tried not to wince as the pain in her ankle suddenly became sharper. "I . . . was trying to keep . . . the . . . Ouch! Sorry . . . nest safe."

Josh had her sock off too, now, and was slowly shaking his head as he looked at the deep bruising beginning to show from her arch up to her shin. "This looks really nasty. I think you had better let me take you home."

"But I haven't finished. If I don't put some more stuff in the way, someone is going to ride through here and run over that nest." Her quick flare of indignation nearly made him laugh, but her effort to climb back down from the truck forced him to take her seriously.

"Just stay put there. What nest?"

"The nest in the road. I nearly hit it myself. That's how I wrecked my bike." Bitsy looked forlornly back toward the crumpled ten-speed, and this time couldn't stop her tears. "I saved all year to be able to buy that bike, and now look at it."

Josh had begun to smile again, but at the onset of Bitsy's tears, he straightened his face in sympathy. "I'll see what I can do. Just stay here for a minute."

Bitsy rested quietly, ignoring the throbbing in her ankle, and watched as Joshua walked back down the dirt road. He looked behind her barrier, crouched down for a few minutes, and then moved off into the woods. He returned lugging a small boulder, which he placed in front of the branches, and then he moved the limbs to form a wide barrier closer to the main road. After a few more branches of his own, Joshua picked up the bicycle and carried it back to the truck.

"That should take care of it." He smiled at her. "Most people won't even bother to try going through here now. After all, what good is a shortcut if it takes more time than the regular road?"

"That's what I thought." She smiled tentatively at him.

"Now let's get you home." He picked her up again, this time lifting her into the high, hard seat in the cab. "You're one of the Traynor kids, aren't you?"

"Yeah." One of the Traynor kids. As always, Bitsy simply disappeared into that vast, undifferentiated mob of Traynor kids. No first name, no identity beyond being one of the middle bunch, nothing to be remembered by. "Yeah. I'm one of the Traynor kids."

Joshua laughed as he started the engine of his truck. "Well, which one are you? I don't think anyone ever introduced you to me."

She narrowed her eyes, wondering if this was a form of teasing she didn't recognize.

"Well? Don't you have a name?"

"Of course I have a name. Don't be an idiot."

He laughed again, liking her spunk. "I wondered if maybe they just called you Number Six or Number Seven."

"Actually, I'm number five."

"You're kidding!" He looked at her in horror until she grinned.

"They don't call me that, silly. My name's Bi . . . Rebecca." She waited for him to contradict her, to tell her that her name was Bitsy, to tell her that little girls should have nicknames.

"How do you do, Rebecca. I'm Josh Mason."

She nodded. "I know."

"So do you always go to so much trouble to protect killdeer?"

"What?"

"Killdeer. The bird." She didn't respond. "That bird whose nest you almost ran over is called a killdeer."

"Why?" She glared at him as if he were personally responsible for misnaming a perfectly innocent creature. "That's seems like a stupid name for a bird. Does it try to kill deer, or something?"

He shook his head and smiled at her. "No. The call they make sounds like the words. Kill-deer! Kill-deer!" He demonstrated the plaintive cry.

His demonstration completely redeemed him in her eyes. "Yes! That's exactly how it sounded. Do you think I hurt it?"

"Why?"

"Because it seemed to be injured. It kind of fluttered around trying to get away from me, and crying all the time."

"That was the father bird just being sneaky, and trying to get you away from the nest."

"You mean acting like a decoy?"

He nodded in approval. "Yep. The birds build their nests right on the ground, and then use themselves as decoys to protect their eggs and young from predators that come around."

"That's really cool! You mean the males do that?"

"The females, too, but the males really know how to put on the show." He thought for a minute and then continued. "They're just like your dad. Last week Brian McCaully started putting the moves on your sister Lauren, and the next thing you know, there's your dad with the hood popped up on Brian's truck talking about revving up the engine. Your mom had Lauren working in the kitchen before Brian ever knew what happened."

Bitsy laughed at this very accurate description of how things operated at the Traynor farm, and she tried to turn to face him in the seat. She pressed her injured foot against the floorboard and nearly yelled in pain. Just in time, she caught herself, gritted her teeth, and gripped hard against the dashboard. Joshua watched her, impressed with her self-control.

"I know your ankle must be hurting a lot," he commented.

"It's not too bad," she replied stoically. "Tell me more about those birds."

He explained how the young birds would hatch quickly and stay hidden on the ground for only a few days before they developed the capacity to fly. "They're quick learners. Then they'll spend the summer fattening up before they migrate south. If the nest is successful, the adults will probably come back near here again next year.''

"Why would they build a nest right out there on the road? Wouldn't it make more sense to hide in the woods, even if they stayed on the ground?''

"There are two ways to look at it. After all, if the predators have trouble seeing the nest, it's also true that the birds have trouble seeing the predators. This way, the birds usually have plenty of time to see anything sneaking up on them, and the adults can try their decoy routine to tempt the enemy away from the nest. Anyway, even in the open, the nest is hard to see, isn't it?''

"Yeah. Hiding right out in the open. It's amazing how easily they can just disappear. . . .'' She let her voice trail off, a slight sadness overcoming the enthusiasm she had shown before.

Josh listened to the wistful tone in her voice and wondered what she was thinking, but they had reached the Traynor home, and he didn't ask her any more questions. Instead, he drove carefully into the drive, watching for bicycles, tricycles, and the tumble of children who ran toward him.

"Hey, Bitsy! Why are you in that truck?''

"What happened?''

"Look at your bike. Mom's gonna kill you!''

"Hi, Josh. What's my little sister done now?''

"Bitsy, Bitsy, are you hurt?''

Josh looked at Rebecca with a twinkle in his eye and asked, "Do you always get a greeting like this?''

But Rebecca had disappeared, to be replaced by Bitsy, and she didn't reply as she hobbled out of the truck. Josh ran around the vehicle as quickly as he could and started to pick her up, but she waved him off.

"I'll be all right, now. Thank you for the ride. Could you help me get my bike down?"

Just then Faye Traynor appeared on the scene, look-ing somewhat frazzled as she wiped one hand on her apron and hoisted her youngest child a little higher on her hip with the other. Within moments Mrs. Traynor had directed Bitsy to the living room sofa, commanded the oldest girls to take the younger children into the backyard, and listened to Josh describe the accident. Bitsy watched through the living room window as her mother spoke with Josh for several minutes. Then with a pang of disappointment she saw him return to his truck and drive off, her ruined bicycle still crumpled on the truck's bed.

In spite of her protests that she was fine, and in spite of her mother's worried comments about the expense, Bitsy found herself X-rayed, bound in a cast, and hob-bling around on crutches. Her father carried her up the long stairway to bed each evening, insisting that she might fall and break the other ankle, but other than that he ignored the accident as just a normal part of life.

The first day following her injury, Bitsy's four older sisters pampered her, urging her to elevate her foot and bringing her the occasional glass of water. By the second day the older girls had lost interest and the four younger sisters took over the nursing duties; however, two-year-old Caitlin and four-year-old Lindsey couldn't do much more than sit beside Bitsy and look sad. By the third day, the older girls were back to asking Bitsy to help them find their lost possessions, and the younger ones insisted that she keep them entertained the way she always did.

She was sitting on the front porch, reading a favorite Beverly Cleary story to eight-year-old Amanda and six-year-old Susan, when she saw the sky-blue pickup pull into the driveway. Joshua stepped out and waved to her before reaching into the back of the truck and lifting out what looked like her bicycle. Bitsy tried to get up, but Lindsey had dragged the crutches to the far end of the porch where she and Caitlin were trying to slide down them. As Bitsy reached for the porch railing to support herself, the front door flew open and sixteen-year-old Colleen raced down the steps toward the truck.

"Hi, Josh! What are you doing here?"

Suddenly the front yard filled with teenage Traynor girls. Lauren and Kelly, only fourteen and thirteen, giggled as they pushed forward to see their latest hero, and even sophisticated Denise, seventeen and almost ready to graduate, lazily moved to flirt with Josh. The rush of young females vying for attention might have resulted in a squabble if the winner hadn't been so obvious. Clearly Colleen had the upper hand. She and Josh were the same age and shared several classes, so her conversation caught and held his attention most easily.

Watching from the railing, Bitsy heaved a sigh of resignation, hopped back to her chair, and picked up her book again. Caitlin climbed into Bitsy's lap, stuck her thumb in her mouth, and snuggled up for a nap. Amanda and Susan begged Bitsy to keep reading, and Lindsey dragged the crutches through the door into the house. Bitsy returned to the book, but she glanced up furtively in the hope of glimpsing her hero from the day before. She thought he looked even more dashing today, his muscles flexed with the weight of the bike he lifted so easily and his shaggy brown hair blowing in the spring breeze.

From the front yard, Josh watched the slender girl leave the railing and disappear behind the pile of younger children who practically fell on her. Her mousy brown hair, light-blue eyes, and sun-tanned limbs dissolved into the camouflage of the brown porch railing and the similar coloring of the other bodies. He smiled, remembering her wistful reaction to the killdeer's camouflage, and began pushing the bike through the mass of older girls.

"Are you up there, Rebecca? I brought your bike back. It was bent some, but I managed to straighten it out for you. I think it will be okay now." He peered up through the porch railing, trying to see her clearly.

"Her name's Bitsy," Susan shouted.

Josh shook his head in disagreement. "Nope. I distinctly remember that her name is Rebecca."

"Nobody calls her Rebecca. Daddy says she's just a Little Bit of a girl. That's why we call her Bitsy."

"Well, dads are allowed to use special nicknames, but friends use the name they're told to use." He smiled as Rebecca stuck her head up to stare at him. "I also brought you a get-well present." He handed her a thick, soft-covered copy of Peterson's *A Field Guide to the Birds*. "I marked the page about the killdeer."

"That was so nice of you," Colleen spoke, touching his arm lightly. "Why don't you come in and have something to drink."

"Yes! Yes! Come on inside." As usual, Lauren and

Kelly spoke practically in unison. "Mom will want to thank you."

They began to drag on his arms, pulling him toward the front steps. Surrounded by admirers, Josh laughed as they manhandled him into the house for lemonade and cookies. He cast one final glance in the direction of Rebecca, but once again he couldn't find her behind all of her siblings. When he left the house half an hour later, Caitlin slept on the floor of the porch, a light blanket tossed over her back. Susan and Lindsey were leaning over the railing using the crutches like giant chopsticks to pick up doll clothes from the ground in front of the porch, and Amanda was reading to herself. Bitsy had disappeared.

Josh thought he saw her pressing her nose to an upstairs window as he backed out of the driveway, and waved in case she was watching him. *What a funny kid,* he thought to himself. *She must get lost in that crowd.*

At the window of the room she shared with Lauren, Kelly, Amanda, and Susan, Bitsy waved back. She rubbed her finger over the inside cover of the book where he had written, *To Rebecca, a natural naturalist.* She smiled to herself and thought, *What a nice boy. He remembered who I am.*

Bob Traynor, walking toward the house from the barn, wiped his sweat- and grease-streaked hands on his overalls and squinted at the blue pickup pulling out of the yard. A father with a brood like his needed to keep an eye on things, even the itsy-bitsy things.

Chapter One

" "That's perfect, Lucinda. What a lovely job you've done." Rebecca patted the older woman's dirt-caked hand with her own equally grimy one. "These will look beautiful next spring."

Lucinda Gray smiled happily, moved her stool a few inches, and began digging another hole in the soft black dirt. She loved the feel of the cool, moist soil between her fingers and digging gave her a satisfaction that kept her calm for hours. It didn't matter that occasionally she would dig eight or nine inches deep instead of the three inches needed for the daffodil bulbs. It also didn't matter that next spring she would not remember having planted the flowers. The brilliant yellow color would surprise and please her just as much as the task of planting pleased her now.

Rebecca moved around the garden, finding another

gardener happily removing the same bulbs he had planted the week before.

"No, Dad! Don't take it out! You're supposed to be putting the bulbs in the ground." Mary Ann Stoner's face registered dismay as she watched her father gently pull the firm white bulb from the hole and place it beside his trowel. She reached for the bulb just as Rebecca knelt beside them.

"It's all right, Mary Ann." She spoke quietly, watching Frank Stoner's face begin to take on the same agitation as his daughter. "It doesn't matter if he takes them out or puts them in. What matters is that he is relaxed and enjoying himself."

Mary Ann bit her lip as her father filled in the hole with the dirt he had just removed. He stopped occasionally to watch the soil sift through his fingers and rub the dirt across his palms. When Rebecca handed him the trowel and guided it back to the earth, he once more began removing the dirt from the hole. Mary Ann sighed heavily, and felt tears sliding down her cheeks.

"I hate this disease," she whispered through her clenched teeth.

Rebecca reached into the cloth bag she had strapped to her waist and pulled out a handful of bulbs. "Here. You plant these yourself. Find a spot you like and just put them in. They should go about two inches apart and three inches deep." She handed the woman a gauge and smiled. "Take your time. See if you can enjoy playing in the dirt as much as your father does."

Mary Ann sighed again. "He does enjoy it, doesn't he?"

"Of course he does. He is living totally in the pres-

ent, and when his present is enjoyable, he can experience a kind of pleasure we can only imagine. No
matter how hard we try, we're not able to get rid of
our worries about the future and our regrets about the
past. Frank doesn't have any of that now. He's beyond
that terrible anxiety of forgetfulness, and now he's living in a kind of purified emotion.''

"I've lost him, though. He's not my father anymore. He doesn't even remember me most of the
time.''

Rebecca dipped her head slightly in a gesture ac-
knowledging Mary Ann's pain, but she also added, "I
don't know about that. I'm not a doctor, and I can't
tell you how much he remembers, but I can see how
he responds to you. He lights up when you're here.
He relaxes more easily. He enjoys this work more.''
She moved with Mary Ann to an empty plot by the
nursing home wall.

"Why don't you plant those here where there's
space?'' Brushing the old mulch out of the way, Rebecca cleared a small plot. "I think he remembers you
on an emotional level, Mary Ann. He doesn't have
coherent thoughts, but he responds to you. Its's as if
his heart remembers what his brain can't.''

Leaving the Stoners, Rebecca joined the aide with
two residents who sat in wheelchairs and planted their
bulbs in a low window box. The two women laughed
and chatted easily with each other. Only someone who
knew them well would realize that much of their conversation contained fabricated information that bore
little resemblance to reality.

"Where's Ben today, Amy?'' Rebecca asked.

"He's having a bad day and they finally sedated
him,'' the young aide replied. "He bruised his arm

real bad when he hit at the nurse this morning."

"I'm sorry to hear that. Maybe he'll be back out here by tomorrow."

After working with the residents in the River Village Nursing Home Alzheimer's Unit for the past six months, Rebecca Traynor felt confident that one bad day didn't necessarily mean a week of them for any patient. That was part of why she loved this work, why she had left the security of her position as a high school biology teacher and started her own business. She had had an uphill battle marketing her own unique brand of horticulture, but hopefully her presentation to the Ohio Department of Natural Resources would be successful tomorrow.

She continued walking the curving path through the enclosed garden and found herself back at Lucinda's plot. The large, quiet woman patted the last of her bulbs and stood up easily. She brushed the dirt from her loose-fitting slacks, and handed her trowel to Rebecca.

"I'm finished," she said with a curt nod, and she headed back to the door into the unit. Rebecca watched until Lucinda was greeted by one of the aides who took her to wash her hands. Each resident was so different. The different stages of their disease interacted with their different personalities until it hardly seemed as if they suffered from the same condition. Lucinda appeared to be the same practical, calm, strong woman she had always been, while poor Ben flailed and fumed with impotent rage at unknown enemies. Rebecca didn't understand all the reasons, but she knew that her gardening worked as a kind of therapy for most of the patients.

Frank continued to dig up his bulbs from last week,

but now Mary Ann sat quietly on the ground beside him. She trailed her fingers through the dirt and watched her father's peaceful expression. Neither of them spoke, but occasionally Mary Ann would touch his arm in a tender gesture. Rebecca knew that the calming effect of working with the soil helped the family members as much as it helped the patients, and she felt grateful that she had been able to give some relief to Mary Ann.

"Will you be back next week?" Amy asked when Rebecca made her final circuit of the garden.

"Of course. I think we'll do fall cleanup then. I have some easy-to-use fan rakes that I think the residents will enjoy. The motions of sweeping and raking are still familiar to most of them. I'll be doing some pruning myself, and I want to let them enjoy the outside as long as possible. Once cold weather sets in, we'll work on our houseplants. I'm hoping we'll have enough things ready to sell at the winter carnival that we can earn money for our spring planting. Part of the therapy is the sense of accomplishment from being as self-sufficient as possible."

Amy nodded in agreement. "We certainly appreciate your work, Rebecca. It makes a lot of difference for the patients. I know you have an ongoing, uphill battle with the administration, but believe me, the staff appreciates your work."

Rebecca held the warm compliment in her heart as she put away the tools in her van and cleaned the final bits of grime from beneath her short fingernails. The autumn sun would remain in the sky long enough for her to make a quick tour of the marsh if she hurried, and Rebecca wanted to look over the site one more time before her presentation in the morning, just to reassure herself that her ideas would work. Shoving her cleaning rag back into one of the built-in drawers she used for such things, Rebecca hopped out of the rear of the vehicle, slammed the door hard enough to force the tricky latch to catch, and climbed into the driver's seat.

By the time she had maneuvered through the Columbus city traffic and reached the country road that would take her to the marsh, she had lost all the benefits of her gardening activities, and her neck and back muscles were taut with stress. Forcing herself to relax again, she bounced along the rough pavement, marveling at how quickly one could leave the metropolitan atmosphere of Columbus and be traveling through farmland and woodland. As much as she disliked the necessity of commuting to Columbus from Delaware County, at least she could still get out of town fairly quickly. Even better was the fact that Columbus still valued plant life, and trees and green spaces abounded even in the center of town.

Slowing the van, she searched for the turnoff to the marshland, and for once spotted the dirt road before she passed it. Situated in a no-man's-land right at the border of Franklin and Delaware counties, the swampy ground sloped to a drainage ditch that carried the water toward the Delaware Reservoir; the land was tangled with underbrush and just begging for thoughtless souls to dump their trash on it. With a little bit of luck, a lot of hard work, and a good plan, Rebecca thought she just might save this place and help some children at the same time.

Dusk hung precariously in the wide sky by the time Rebecca parked on the edge of the dirt road, and she feared that night would actually fall before she could make her last survey of the area. Quickly she pulled a set of drawings from the small portfolio on the passenger's seat and grabbed a flashlight from her glove compartment, then she followed the minimal path through the woods to the edge of the murky waterway.

Not quite a stream, but more than just wet ground, with the proper landscaping the natural drainage path could be coaxed into ponds so that the water levels could be managed deliberately. Rebecca's hopes for this park included two full ponds, with controlled water levels, a variety of plant species native to the area that would help maintain the marsh characteristics, and a rather unique boardwalk which would allow wheelchair access to the site without damage to the foliage. She looked at her drawings, and compared them with the dark, tangled wilderness before her, hoping that what she had seen in the daylight more closely resembled her plans than this nighttime jungle.

A loud snapping sound behind her made her jump— suddenly she was aware that she was completely alone in these woods. She had never seen another person here, and she had forgotten to take even the minimal precaution of telling anyone where she was going. Her heart pounded hard against her chest as she heard another twig popping with the pressure of something's weight, and she switched off her flashlight as a precaution.

"Hello?" A man's voice, deep but not threatening, called out. "Are you lost?"

Rebecca's throat closed and she couldn't answer even if she had wanted to do so. Should she run? Should she remain absolutely still? Even during daylight, this was hardly the kind of ground for easy running. In the darkness, she would most likely break her neck before she went ten yards.

A lantern shone through the woods, bobbing slightly with the movement of the person carrying it. ''Hello!'' This time the word carried a bit more force, something authoritative. ''I'm sorry, but this is restricted city property. You're not supposed to be here. I'll be happy to help you find your way out, if you're lost.''

She breathed a sigh of relief. No one would sound so officious unless he actually worked for the government. She turned her own flashlight on again and guided her feet back along the path.

''I'm not lost,'' she called. ''And I have permission to be here. Who are you?''

''I work for City Parks and Rec,'' came the answer as he held his lantern higher, making it a beacon as she moved closer, and then continuing to hold it high as she moved into the circle of light.

He was so tall that even though he held the lantern well over her head, his own features were hidden in the darkness above the hooded light. Like a spotlight, the brightness blinded her, making it impossible to see him clearly, but she had an impression of leanness as well as height. Unlike most of the park employees he did not wear a uniform but sported old blue jeans and a flannel shirt.

''What are you doing here?'' he asked, the friendliness once again tempering the authority in his tone.

''I'm Rebecca Traynor. I'm working on a proposed development of this land that I'm going to present tomorrow morning to your department and ODNR. I was just checking out the site one last time.''

''Rebecca Traynor? I . . .'' He brought the lamp

even closer to her face. "I . . . you're working out here? I see." He hesitated. "I'm . . . uh . . . are you finished? I mean, it's pretty dark to be doing much out here." He seemed to have lost his commanding voice for the moment, as if he didn't quite know whether to leave her alone or insist that she go away.

Rebecca slapped at a late mosquito and sighed. "You're right. There's not much more I can do, anyway. I was just trying to calm my last-minute jitters. I'll get out of your way." She realized that she did feel like an interloper. Until now, she had thought of this as her marsh, and the project as already hers, but this man's presence reminded her that nothing about the grant was assured.

"You're certainly not in my way," he replied hastily. "In fact, I'm already finished. I just wouldn't want to leave you alone here in the dark. It's pretty isolated."

"It's all right," she insisted as she started walking back to the van. "I really can't do much now." Curious about his presence here at this hour, she asked, "What about you? What are you doing here? I've never seen anyone else out here before."

"That's probably because you can't do your work in the dark, but a lot of mine is done then."

"Really? What do you do?"

"Don't you . . . I mean, I'm an entomologist. I'm doing some wildlife studies out here, and I sometimes come at night to make bat and insect counts."

Rebecca slapped another mosquito and wiped its flattened remains off her leg. "Well, don't count that one, it's not here anymore."

He laughed and held the lamp even higher to illu-

minate a fallen log in their path. "Don't worry, there
are plenty more of those."

They reached the clearing where the dirt road
started, and Rebecca saw his truck with the official
city seal on the side. With a sigh of relief, she realized
she hadn't been absolutely certain about him until
then.

"Be careful on your way back to the highway," the
tall man said as he pulled open the door for her. "I
had to wait for five deer at one point, and they weren't
in any hurry to cross the road."

He seemed anxious for her to leave, and she
clamped down on her rebellious streak that would
have had her remain longer simply to prove that she
had the right to do so. As she hoisted herself into the
high seat of her van, he lowered the lantern, finally
removing his face from the protection of the glare and
revealing his serious countenance in the warm glow
of the van light. Rebecca stared into his dark brown
eyes, they were large and wide-set, with laugh lines
clearly visible and contrasting with his deeply tanned
skin. Those laugh lines suggested that most of the time
he was more sociable than he acted this evening. His
face was angular, thinness emphasizing the strong
bones of his cheeks and jaw, and the slight shadowing
of his day's growth of beard adding to the sharpness
rather than softening it.

The jolt of recognition hit her sharply, and she
sucked in a quick breath. Rebecca knew he must be
nearly thirty now, obviously a man of strength and
experience; his lean, well-muscled arm rested easily
on the hood of the van as he watched her curiously.
She blushed, not with the realization that she had been
staring, but with the awkwardness and immaturity she

suddenly felt, and the unexpected hurt. With that one glimpse of his face, Rebecca lost thirteen years of her life and regressed to the gawky, infatuated child she had been the first time she saw this man's eyes up close, and she silently cursed herself for never managing to overcome her feelings for Joshua Mason.

With unaccustomed irritability, Rebecca slammed her door shut, revved the engine a few times, and squealed her tires as she backed away from Josh. He jerked his hand away from the vehicle and jumped out of the way as she tried to make a U-turn on the narrow road. She lost even more dignity as she realized the turning radius of the van was so great that she would have to back up at least two more times before she could head out of the wilderness area, and by the time she completed her circle, Joshua stood in front of her with his hands held up to stop her.

"Are you all right?" he asked her, bewilderment showing clearly on his face.

"I'm fine," she answered, wishing desperately that he couldn't see her inflamed cheeks. "I just realized how late it is, and I'm in a big hurry. Sorry to have disturbed your bug hunting." He stepped away from the van again, and this time she managed to drive out of the park at a sedate pace rather than like the proverbial bat out of the underworld.

He didn't even remember me, she thought with a moan as she pulled onto the highway and sped along the reservoir toward home. *Of course he didn't remember me. What an idiot I am. Why would he remember some scrawny little kid who used to hide out behind her sisters just to get a glimpse of him?* She knew this description painted an unfair picture of both of them, but it was the image that had carried her through a long disappointing time, and she clung to it now.

Swerving to avoid a raccoon in the middle of the road, Rebecca felt the weight in the back of the van shifting, and she slowed down to something closer to the speed limit. The action brought her back to her senses, and she realized just how out of control she had been. This wasn't like her. She was the sensible one of the Traynor girls: never emotional, always competent and compassionate, the one everyone depended on. Gradually her emotions slid back out of her awareness into those safely locked mental cupboards where she kept them.

Slowing the old Chevy even more, she wondered if the Rototiller had broken free from its moorings, a circumstance that had caused her plenty of headaches on more than one occasion. She tried the brakes cautiously, feeling and hearing the ominous scrape across the back floor. All she wanted now was to get home and soak in a hot bath, but if anything happened to her tools before she made it home, her entire livelihood would be in danger. With a sigh, she maneuvered the van off the highway, once again climbed into the back, and methodically braced the heavy tiller back in place against the wall.

When she started down the road again, Rebecca noticed another city truck parked in a lay-by a few hundred yards past the spot where she had stopped. *This must be a busy night for city employees*, she thought as the other truck waited until she passed and then pulled out behind her. She wondered again about the coincidence of meeting Josh Mason out at her marsh, and spent the rest of her drive laughing at herself for expecting anyone to remember her after so many years.

Meanwhile Josh watched the van rush down the rough drive away from the marsh, and then he stooped to gather his equipment into his truck. She certainly wanted to get away quickly, but he supposed that only made sense. A beautiful young woman, alone in a dark, isolated spot with a man she didn't know . . . didn't remember. Perhaps if he had reminded her that she knew him years ago, she wouldn't have been so frightened, but he felt more than a little self-conscious about how well he remembered her.

Bouncing with every pothole, Josh thought that maybe development of this area wouldn't be such a bad idea, if it meant scraping this road smooth. Then he glanced at his catch of insects for the night and realized he would fight the changes even if the road became completely impassable. He had hoped to find stronger indications of a resurgent population of insects after the warm wet summer, but the marshland seemed barely to hold its own; any new development in this area would surely spell disaster for the entire ecology of the place.

Josh turned onto the highway with a sigh. Why would Rebecca Traynor want to civilize this swampy wilderness? She had always loved the wildlife of the area. She had even insisted on helping him his senior year of high school when he had spent hours at the reservoir studying the zebra mussels. He realized he didn't really know her anymore, hadn't talked to her for years, in spite of the fact that he had occasionally observed her from a distance, and she might be very different from the child he had once liked so much.

Physically she had changed a great deal in the years since they had known each other. Her mousy brown hair had darkened to a rich chestnut color, and it framed her strong face with thick waves. Her eyes were still pale blue, but they had flashed a challenge at him, at least until she suddenly ran away. Her figure now matched what the older Traynor sisters had been like. All in all, he thought, she had turned out pretty much the way he expected.

He knew he was following her route and he was watching for her taillights when he realized she had pulled off the road. Her van stood empty and silent on the side of the road, the lettering PERSONAL TRAYNOR showing up against the ridiculously flowered background, and Josh would have slammed on the brakes to help her, but for the memory of her wide-eyed stare and urgent desire to get away from him. Instead he slowed his truck and found another pull-off just ahead of her where he waited for a few minutes, watching for her in his rearview mirror. When her headlights came back on and she passed him, he let out the breath he had unconsciously been holding.

Old habits die hard, he thought to himself as he watched her van make the final turn to the Traynor farm. *And watching out for Rebecca Traynor is a very old habit.*

Chapter Two

"Bitsy! Bitsy! Bitsy!" The thin, high wail of the six-year-old-girl's voice grated against Rebecca's sleep-drugged mind, and she wanted to reach out and shake the child into silence. Instead, she sat up calmly and held out her hand.

"Patty." Rebecca spoke firmly, trying to pull the child's attention away from her own noise. "Patty, come here."

Tangled hair waving as she fiercely shook her head, Patty continued to stand at the end of the bed, shout at her aunt, and ignore the outstretched hand. "Bitsy! Bitsy! Bitsy! Bitsy!" The words acted not as a link between the child and woman, but as a wall of sound that served only to separate them from each other.

"*Patty!*" Rebecca finally shouted louder than her flailing niece and snapped her fingers in the child's face. Patty shut her mouth in sudden compliance.

26

Rebecca held out her hand once again, and this time Patty moved along the side of the bed to stand at Rebecca's side without looking at her. "Hello, Patty." Rebecca returned to the firm, soft tone with which she had begun.

"Bitsy," Patty responded, still slightly louder than necessary, but at least not shouting.

"Thank you, Patty." Rebecca swung her legs off the bed and grabbed the robe she had thrown down the night before. "Have you eaten your breakfast?"

"Breakfast . . . breakfast . . . BREAKFAST . . . *BREAKFAST!*" Patty marched out the bedroom door, her words, emphatic but slightly slurred, once again catching an unstoppable rhythm that propelled her along without thought and without awareness. With a brief but heartfelt prayer for patience, Rebecca followed Patty down the stairs to the large kitchen.

"It's going to be a difficult day," Mrs. Traynor lamented as she handed Rebecca a cup of coffee. "I don't know how you're going to manage her today."

Rebecca guided Patty to the computer desk in the corner of the dining room and turned on a simple, nonverbal game while trying to listen to her mother over Patty's continuing shouts. A corral of bookcases provided an effective barrier from other stimulants, and after several minutes Patty finally became engrossed in the game. Her shouts decreased in volume and frequency. She continued to speak to herself and to ignore the others when they spoke, but at least she didn't completely disrupt all conversation. Gradually, Rebecca eased herself out of the computer corner and into the large kitchen.

"Where is Colleen?" Rebecca asked, slicing toast

and stuffing it into the toaster. "Doesn't she ever watch her own daughter anymore?"

"Don't be uncharitable," her mother rebuked her gently. "Colleen and Chuck took Shelly to visit Chuck's mother this week. You knew they were going. I don't know what's on your mind these days, Bitsy, but you just can't seem to remember anything."

"Mom, I have a very important presentation to make to the Ohio Department of Natural Resources this morning. I told you about it weeks ago. I can't possibly watch Patty today."

"Come on, Mom, let's go!" Caitlin and Lindsey dashed into the room, slinging bookbags and canvas luggage over their shoulders and grabbing their brown-bag lunches like synchronized swimmers. "See you later, Bits."

"Mom," Rebecca pleaded, "I can't watch her today. If I don't get this grant, I'm not going to earn enough money to keep my business going this year. I'm not going to make any kind of financial contribution to this household."

"Oh, Bitsy, this *is* your contribution. I just don't think she'll be able to stay at the preschool today. You see how she is, and you're the only one who can do this. I'm sorry, but it's too late to make any other arrangements."

"But, Mom . . ." Rebecca protested, but she felt her resistance crumbling.

"Come on, Mom. We're going to be late. Mr. Lucas said they wouldn't hold the bus for anyone who's late. We'll miss the trip if you don't hurry!" The two youngest Traynor girls glowed with adolescent excitement and Rebecca felt her heart pulled with an almost maternal pride.

"I'm sorry," Mrs. Traynor repeated. "We'll be back Friday night. The doctor's number is on the refrigerator if she gets any worse, but I'm sure you'll manage her the way you always do. You are my dependable one." With a kiss on Rebecca's cheek, Mrs. Traynor picked up her own bags and followed her two youngest daughters out the door.

Rebecca stared after the retreating automobile, and wondered desperately what she would do to control her autistic niece during the formal presentation this morning. Frustrated, she imagined Colleen and her husband Chuck relaxing on the lakefront deck of his mother's house while they watched their younger daughter, the perfect, beautiful Shelly, play happily with her dolls and crayons. But Rebecca's irritation couldn't compete with the inevitable sense of contentment she had whenever her family depended on her, and she tried to face the day stoically.

"Bitsy! Bitsy! No . . . no . . . no!" Patty slammed a fist down on the keyboard and then howled even more loudly at the pain.

"Come on, Patty." Rebecca swallowed a new wave of frustration and redirected her niece again. "Come and work in the dirt for me, while I get dressed," she entreated.

"No . . . !" Patty continued yelling and fell limply when Rebecca took her hand.

"Come on." Rebecca tried again. Patiently she picked the thin girl off the floor and carried her into the laundry room where Rebecca kept ready a small flower box. Patty's rigid form and renewed complaints didn't portend a successful transition, but fortunately the flower box provided an attractive diversion. Rebecca glanced around the room to make certain no one had left any running appliances, and then allowed Patty to find her own way to the flower box. Within minutes the child immersed herself in the new activity.

With a plastic shovel and a few bulbs, Patty busily planted and replanted the flowers in a miniature version of Frank Stoner's behavior, while Rebecca quickly donned a pair of slacks and a matching jacket that were hanging in the laundry room. Rushing into the bathroom to brush her teeth and fix her hair, Rebecca prayed again that Patty would stay out of trouble long enough to allow her aunt to finish dressing.

Finally, Rebecca slid quietly back behind her niece and began the difficult job of untangling the child's hair without igniting Patty's frenzy at being touched. Amazingly, Patty continued to hum softly to herself and run the fine, soft soil through her fingers while Rebecca brushed and braided the mass of brown curls. If she hadn't feared Colleen's wrath, Rebecca would have cut off all of Patty's locks and avoided this daily hassle.

"Okay, kid, let's go."

"Go. No. Go. No." Patty agreed, picking up a handful of dirt from the box.

"Honey, you can't take that with—" Rebecca began, but Patty stared at the floor and tightened her grip on the dirt that continued to seep through her fingers. In desperation, Rebecca acquiesced. "Okay. We'll take the dirt, but in the box, and you have to put the lid on while we're driving."

Nearly an hour later, Patty trailed behind while Rebecca carried the box of dirt and a briefcase full of landscape designs into the hearing room in the ODNR office. Two other applicants awaited their turns while a third completed a plea for more playground equipment for an urban park on the city's south side. Amazingly, Patty sat in one of the chairs, opened the box, and played quietly with her dirt while the presentations continued, but Rebecca watched her with such trepidation that she hardly noticed the room's other occupants.

Finally her turn arrived, and Rebecca stood to face the panel of officers who would either deny her project or grant her the funding to fulfill the dream she had been pursuing the past two years. She opened her mouth to explain her vision and quickly shut it again. There, just slightly apart from the three hearing officers, sat Joshua Mason, looking unfamiliarly formal in a suit and tie. He didn't look at her, but studied his copy of the prospectus she had mailed in several weeks ago.

"Ms. Traynor?" The presiding officer watched her curiously. "Are you ready?"

Rebecca forced herself back to business. "Yes, ma'am. If you would like to open your packets to page three, I think I can give you the quickest explanation of my proposal by detailing the outline there." Now Rebecca was into her memorized speech, and she easily covered her ideas.

The marshland on the border of the county currently stood unused and unappreciated by the public who owned it. The twelve acres of swamp and wood could not be accessed because of the lack of trails, and the vegetation grew too thickly to allow much variety of plant and animal wildlife. With the proper design and management, the area could include a number of different habitats.

"But the aspect of my plan that makes it unique is

that much of the initial work and upkeep on this land would be done by special high school students.''

"We have a number of science classes from our school districts that already conduct ecology projects in our parks, Ms. Traynor,'' replied the president.

"But I mean that this work would be done by students with certain handicaps,'' Rebecca answered. "If we make the area wheelchair accessible, these students will have an opportunity that is usually denied them.''

Rebecca directed their attention to the extensive list of research papers that indicated that intensive, hands-on activities helped children who could not work well in the typical classroom environment. The American Horticultural Therapy Association had begun amassing a significant amount of data that supported the claims that horticultural activities helped a wide variety of people with physical and emotional difficulties. With her own credentials as a teacher, Rebecca felt certain that she could operate the project successfully, and the hearing officers seemed to be agreeing with her.

"What about the already fragile condition of that area?'' a slow, serious voice asked. "I've been studying that wetland for a year now, and I don't think it can stand much stress. I think if you start putting in boardwalks and cutting down vegetation, you may just make the entire ecosystem collapse.''

Rebecca's heart sank. She had hoped that Josh's presence meant he would support her idea, but apparently he had come here today to oppose her. Could he actually have forgotten her? She realized she didn't know him at all anymore. Perhaps he had transformed into someone who didn't care about things the way she did.

"I haven't been studying the area for a full year

yet,'' she said, attempting to sound less desperate than she felt, ''but I think the changes would actually help the ecosystem. I know that there would be some temporary stress, but in the long run, the vegetation would be much healthier. It's like pruning a bush to make it come back stronger.''

The three officers turned back to Josh waiting for a reply. ''Dr. Mason?'' the president asked. ''Do you agree?''

Josh folded his hands on top of Rebecca's prospectus. ''It's an impressive project, Ms. Traynor, and I think it has some merit, but caring for the entire system is not the same as simply pruning a bush. You certainly know horticulture and educational theory, but I don't believe you're quite as strong in zoology. There are a number of fairly delicate animal species in the park that might not survive the wholesale demolition of the area, even if that demolition is only temporary. By the time your pruning takes effect, these species may have permanently disappeared from the scene.''

''Do you mean extinction, Dr. Mason? Are there any endangered species living in the marsh?'' the chairwoman asked.

''Well, I've identified two rare species of warblers there,'' Mason replied. ''I don't say that we would be responsible for endangering the species if we go through with this project, but I do say that we need to be very careful of when and how we make changes.'' He spoke so seriously that Rebecca felt as if he were a total stranger. With a burst of indignation she wondered if this man cared about his birds more than he cared about the children she wanted to help.

''I assure you, I don't want to do anything harmful,'' Rebecca defended herself. ''I think that land is in danger right now. You may be monitoring that site, but no one takes care of it, and I know that it's going to turn into an unofficial dump soon, if it isn't more obviously protected.'' She spoke directly to Josh, willing him to bend his severity just a little.

He smiled suddenly, and Rebecca remembered a hundred times during her childhood when that smile had signaled Josh Mason's approval of one of her ideas. He beamed at her now as if she were a difficult student who had just shown a previously unsuspected talent.

''I understand that you need the special ramps and raised earth beds in order to make the area accessible to your students, but I'm concerned about what this construction might do to the animals already living there. I don't think it's impossible, though.'' He turned to speak to the chairwoman. ''I would suggest one change to Ms. Traynor's project, and then I would give it my wholehearted support.''

''What?'' Rebecca asked simultaneously with the three hearing officers.

''I suggest that she and I combine our projects. The Columbus Department of Parks and Recreation hired me as a wildlife manager, and I've been monitoring that area and several other undeveloped parklands. I suggest that we add myself as a consultant to her development plans, with the proviso that if we uncover any problems with the animal wildlife, she will slow or reverse the changes she has made. We'll work together to ensure that the animal species aren't endangered.''

The hearing officers conferred among themselves for a few minutes before the president spoke. ''Ms.

Traynor, we believe that your proposal has exceptional merit and want to consider it for funding; however, our policy for several years has been to grant primacy to preserving endangered wildlife habitats from any change. Since Dr. Mason has supervised the implementation of this policy in the Columbus parks, we believe he must also supervise your project. We will accept your proposal for possible budgeting if you will accept the addition of Dr. Mason as project supervisor.''

Rebecca didn't know what to say. She had developed this idea from nothing, and she certainly hadn't intended to have someone else step in at the last minute to oversee all of her work. Of course she knew that any government funding came with paperwork and accountability, but this arrangement would place the project under Josh Mason's name. Somehow it felt like a replay of most of her life: Rebecca Traynor did a great deal of work, someone else got the credit, and in the end no one even remembered her name.

Suddenly the stillness of the hearing room was shattered. One of the other applicants had remained in the room to listen to Rebecca's presentation and he had become fascinated with Patty's digging. Innocently he reached over and touched her hand to get her attention.

''*No!*'' she shouted in a voice that held none of its earlier irritability but still could shatter the nerves of the uninitiated. ''*No!*''

Rebecca smiled in resignation as the three panelists raised their eyebrows. ''I apologize for the interruption. My niece has a handicap of her own that makes sitting quietly difficult for her.''

''NO!'' Patty raised the emotional pitch a few decibels and Rebecca felt the tension in the room begin to rise.

All of her own resistance collapsed with Patty's rising agitation, and Rebecca realized she didn't care who received credit for the project as long as she got the funding. Whatever it took to keep this project going, Rebecca would do it.

"I'm willing to work under Dr. Mason's supervision," she answered as she gathered her papers and moved back to Patty's side before there was any chance that the dirt box would go flying across the room. "Do I need to rewrite the proposal, or can I just accept your changes?"

"Dr. Mason will be in touch with you, Ms. Traynor," the president spoke as she and her colleagues packed up their own materials to leave for lunch.

"Bitsy!" Patty was becoming more and more insistent even while Rebecca hurriedly crammed papers in her briefcase so she could get her away, but suddenly the child held absolutely still and stared mesmerized past Rebecca's shoulder. "Rabbit!"

Josh held the knotted white handkerchief behind his arm to create the impression of bunny ears slowly rising and quickly lowering again. Rebecca flashed him a grateful smile and lifted the dirt box away from Patty while the child continued to watch the bunny ears. If Patty ever smiled, Rebecca thought it would be now, at the sight of the tantalizing, floppy ears moving up and down behind the man's arm. But, of course, Patty didn't smile; she simply stared with her large, solemn eyes.

"Watch now," Josh whispered and he flipped the handkerchief open to show Patty what he had used.

Patty didn't shout or demonstrate her consternation

in any way. She didn't look at Josh or Rebecca. Instead she looked down at the floor and made tiny rocking movements with her torso.

"Let's go home, Patty, and see your own bunny rabbit," Rebecca said cheerfully, hoping to head off any more explosions.

"Home," Patty responded with unexpected compliance. She followed Josh out the door, and Rebecca brought up the rear.

When they reached the street, Rebecca expected to say a quick good-bye to Josh, but instead he lifted the box from her arms and told her to lead the way. They made an interesting parade as they dodged the other pedestrians along Broad Street: Josh with the portable garden, Rebecca with her briefcase bulging with papers, and Patty with her singsong repetition of the word "Go." They trooped to Rebecca's van, where Josh deposited the box and vanished before Rebecca had time to do more than say a brief thank-you.

She assumed he still didn't remember her.

Chapter Three

Shutting the bedroom door softly, Rebecca held her breath with the fear that Patty would once again rouse and become agitated instead of remaining asleep. Rationally, Rebecca knew that the slight squeak of the carpeted stairs would not actually awaken her niece, but the child frequently resumed her howling before Rebecca made it back down the stairs, and the aunt had become stealthy in an attempt to slip away from the lengthy bedtime rituals. Fortunately, tonight Patty remained quiet as Rebecca descended to the living room.

"So, are you happy about your new garden project?" her father asked without setting the newspaper down.

"Of course! If they provide the funding I should be able to start work before winter, if we can get the equipment out there to dig the ponds and the access ramps. Of course, it's not exactly a garden; it's a wild-life preserve.''

''It sounds like a lot of work. Are you sure you can handle it all?''

''Dad, it's what I want to do more than anything else. I'm a registered horticultural therapist, and I own my own business. Of course I can handle it.''

''Hmm.''

Rebecca shrugged, futilely assuming he hadn't actually listened to her, and began stacking the dishes before washing them. With her mother and two youngest sisters away for the high school trip to Washington, D.C., Rebecca had only to cook and clean up after herself, her father, and Patty. The house seemed strangely empty with all of her siblings gone.

The telephone rang shrilly in the silence, and Rebecca raced to answer it before the noise awoke Patty.

''Bitsy, hi!'' Lauren's familiar laughter chased away the silence. ''Is Mom there?''

''Sorry, Lauren. She's off to D.C. with Lindsey and Caitlin.''

''Oh, well, what about Colleen?''

''Nope. She and Chuck are at the lake.''

''Is Denise there?''

''Lauren, no one is here except Dad and Patty. He's reading the paper and she's gone to bed.''

''Oh. That must be bizarre . . . well, then, never mind. Kelly and Rich are here and we thought the four of us might come over, but if no one's home, I guess we'll just stay here. When are Mom and the kids coming home?''

''Friday—'' Rebecca heard the doorbell chime and listened for her father's footsteps before she continued with her sister. "You know, Dad and I are somebody, Lauren."

"Oh, well, you know what I mean. Rich and Tim won't want to come if Chuck and Mike aren't there, and Kelly and I can see you anytime."

Voices, her father's and someone else's, carried down the hallway into the kitchen.

"Someone's here, Lauren. Dad just answered the door, so I'd better go see what it is. It's probably someone selling something, and you know how Dad is sometimes."

Her father's voice sounded closer. ". . . just back in the kitchen. Here she is. Bits, look who's come to visit us."

"Who is it, Bitsy?" Lauren asked excitedly, obviously hearing the conversation over the phone.

"You remember Josh Mason, don't you, Bits?"

"Josh Mason! Oh, wow," Lauren screeched into Rebecca's ear. "I haven't seen him for ages. Is he as cute as ever, Bitsy? What's he doing there? Is he going to stay for a while? Maybe Tim and I will come over after all. Ask him if he'll wait."

Rebecca stood immobile with the receiver a few inches away from her ear, protecting herself from the high-pitched questions continuing to stream from her sister's mouth but unable to attend to either Lauren or her father. Ducking his head slightly to hide his understanding grin, Josh watched her struggle for some control of the situation.

"I'll call you back later, Lauren."

"Wait! We're coming o . . ." Gently Rebecca replaced the receiver in the cradle and swiveled back to face the two men, her glance vacillating from one to the other.

"You remember Josh, Bits. He used to hang out with that crowd your sisters ran around with. But maybe they were too old for you," her father continued. "Those days were a lot of fun, weren't they, Josh? Four pretty girls and a swarm of boys hovering around like bees after honey. I used to wonder if I ought to chase you all off with a shotgun."

Josh had been smiling at Rebecca while her father spoke, but now he returned his attention to the older man. "This was always a nice place to hang out, Mr. Traynor."

"Oh, call me Bob, Josh. You're hardly a kid anymore. Come on out to the front porch and sit a spell while the weather's still so nice. Bitsy, do we have anything to drink?"

She nodded, still too off guard to know what to say, and opened the refrigerator for the pitcher of lemonade.

"Can I help?" Josh offered quietly.

"Oh, that's all right. Bitsy can get it," Bob replied as he started back to the front of the house. "She's real handy in the kitchen."

"Can I help?" Josh asked, even more quietly, asking Rebecca alone, not her father.

She shook her head and finally managed to say, "It's all right. I'll bring it out in a minute." She ignored the thought that he had always been more concerned about her feelings than anyone else had ever been; such thoughts had already led to too many wasted years. She poured the cold liquid into three plastic Tupperware cups—nothing fancy for some old friend of her sisters—and caught her breath when he reached around her to take two of them.

"There's no use doing things the hard way, when

a little help makes things easy,'' he stated with a little shake of his head as he stood back for her to lead the way to the front porch.

"What are you up to these days?" Bob asked when Josh and Rebecca had seated themselves on the old porch swing facing him. "I can't recall you coming by for a visit for quite a while."

"Didn't Rebecca tell you?" Josh looked at her with some speculation. "We're going to be working together on a project in that old swampland on the south side of the reservoir."

Josh waited for Rebecca to explain, but when she continued to sit quietly sipping her lemonade he proceeded to describe in detail all that she planned to do.

"Well, that's just great," Bob finally replied. "And Bitsy's going to help you, is she? Well, that's real nice of you. Why didn't you tell me, Bits?" She would have explained that she had already told him and that the project was her own, but he didn't even wait for her to reply. "I seem to remember you used to traipse around after Josh quite a lot when you were just a little kid, Bitsy. Going to pick up the habit again?"

"That's been a while, Dad." Rebecca groaned.

"I think Rebecca will be in the lead for this project," Josh inserted, hoping to change the unfortunate course of the conversation. "I'm just watching out for my wildlife."

"You always were real careful about those smaller and weaker than you, Josh," Bob replied and then went on. "I know Faye will be real sorry she missed you. She's gone on the high school trip to Washington with the two babies."

"Babies?" Josh raised his eyebrows.

"Lindsey and Caitlin," Rebecca answered. "They're seventeen and fifteen now."

"I know. I remember."

"Yep. They're growing up to be fine young women. You know my grown girls are all married now. All four of them."

Josh revealed nothing, but he could practically hear Rebecca crackle as her body fixed with rigidity. Grown girls indeed. He pushed himself up off the swing and set his glass down on the porch rail. "I hate to let business interfere with pleasure, Bob, but I need to talk to Rebecca about her project before I go." He held out his hand to help her up. "Can we take a walk?"

"Sure." She spoke without a trace of the relief she felt.

"You do what Josh tells you, Bitsy. I'm sure you'll be able to handle the work if you just pay close attention to what he tells you to do."

"Okay, Dad. I'll do that." She wondered if her father even remembered that she had graduated from the university with honors and had been her sister Susan's biology teacher for a year. She wondered if he even noticed how her eyes glazed over and her tone became light and airy whenever she was furious with his condescension.

"Come on, Rebecca," Josh urged her with a tug on her hand. "Let's go take that walk before someone gets frostbite."

He pulled her along into the darkness, and didn't let go of her hand even after they reached the edge of the cornfield. Drying ears of field corn lay scattered among the broken, yellow-brown stalks, reminding Rebecca of Halloweens when she had gathered these leftovers into decorations for her sisters' parties. In the wonder of suddenly finding herself here with her old friend, she shook off the resentment she had been fighting all day.

"What did you mean about frostbite?" she asked.

Josh squeezed her fingers and laughed. "You haven't really changed all that much, you know. I could always hear that coldness in your voice. You get too terribly nice and lighthearted, when what you want deep down is to knock somebody's teeth loose!"

She laughed, too, relishing the sudden freedom from the day's anger and nearly breathless with happiness that he could act as if they had always been friends.

"Did you really forget me?" He asked the question suddenly and with a skepticism that denied the possibility.

"Forget you?" she stalled.

"Last night . . . you looked so frightened, and you left so suddenly, I thought you must not have remembered me at all. And then today you didn't say anything." He dropped her hand and hefted an ear of the corn.

"I . . ." If she admitted that she remembered him, she'd have to explain why she had run off so quickly without even saying hello. "You . . ."

"It's all right." Suddenly he relented and gave her the easy out. "It doesn't hurt my ego too awfully. I could hardly expect you to know me after ten years."

"It's only been eight years. You came back the third summer after you started college. But Colleen was engaged to Chuck by then, so I guess you figured it wasn't a good idea to keep coming around."

"Ah. So you do remember me." He couldn't tell her that he had had another reason why it wasn't a good idea to keep coming back. His father had warned him, quite vociferously, that twenty-one-year-old men who spent too much time in the company of sixteen-year-old girls could be called many things, none of them nice.

"What did you want to talk about?" Rebecca couldn't concentrate on anything except the lonely feeling in her fingers when he had released her hand, and she knew she needed to focus on something before she acted like the child she had once been.

"Hmm?" Josh was peeling the corn with extraordinarily deliberate movements.

"You said you wanted to talk about the project?"

"Oh. Right." He twisted the corn, apparently trying to wring oil from the puckered kernels. "I wanted to apologize for what happened today."

"Apologize?" She felt tremendously stupid. "Today?"

He dropped the corn and faced her squarely. "Look. I didn't mean to take over your project. I just wanted to warn you about the fragility of some of the species there. I thought we could collaborate. I would never try to take over someone else's work . . . especially not yours. I didn't expect them to put you under my supervision." He knew he was rambling; he couldn't tell if he had started groveling yet. "I thought it might actually be fun to work together again. I don't want you to be angry with me." Now he knew he was groveling.

"I'm not angry."

"That's the voice."

"What voice?"

"The one you use when you wish you could erupt

like Mt. Vesuvius and you don't want anyone to know it.''

In the distance she could see a pair of headlights turning off the road and onto the long gravel drive to the house, and she realized that Lauren and Kelly had arrived. Too soon. She never had enough time.

"So?" He waited for her to respond to some question, but she had forgotten what it was.

"Lauren and Kelly are here, probably with their husbands. They want to see you.''

"I didn't come to see them, Rebecca. I came to talk to you about the project. I want to be able to help you, I want to support your work, but I don't want you to resent me.''

"Of course I don't resent you. I'm grateful to have the project considered at all. It was very generous of you to support me the way you did.'' She smiled ever so politely.

He gritted his teeth with frustration as he heard her slip into the acquiescing role of Bitsy, the selfless member of the Traynor clan. He understood that she used the role to survive in this hive of too many queens. She didn't fight, or demand; she didn't use humor (although she could be very funny) or flirt outrageously. She was quiet and shy, tender, compassionate, and a devilish hard worker, and she held her one tiny niche in this family by taking care of the others and never admitting it if she resented things. This was the first time he had ever known her to use that role with him, but then he hadn't been around for a long time.

"Bitsy!" Lauren's voice echoed across the field, hitting the old barn and moving on.

"This sounds like old times. Don't they ever let you

have time for yourself?'' He needed to finish this conversation before she was pulled away once more.

''You know what this family is like, Josh. My parents have nine daughters, four sons-in-law, five grand-
children, and two more on the way. We all share the
work, or it doesn't get done.'' She smiled the polite
smile again and started toward the house, but he
reached for her hand and held her back.

''Rebecca, I meant what I said. I don't want you to
resent me.''

Rebecca ruthlessly shoved down the involuntary
emotions sparked by his touch. It was an old feeling:
something left over from long ago, something from
her anxious, awkward adolescence. With an effort she
found an adult response. She sighed and smiled, a
small but at least genuine smile.

''I don't resent you, Josh. I understand why they
wanted to put you in charge, and I'll get over the disappointment in a day or so.'' Finally she grinned, the
old familiar crinkling of a mischievous imp. ''Just
don't act too cocky and we'll do fine.''

Rebecca was back and Bitsy once again banished to
deal with others. ''Good.'' He sounded relieved.
''Then I'll see you at the site day after tomorrow. If
you can get those ponds started before winter it will
give the migratory warblers a better chance for nesting
next spring, so we'd better get the construction crew
out there with the backhoe by next week.''

''They funded me?''

''Of course.''

''They funded me!''

''Bitsy!'' Once again Lauren's call broke into the
stillness of the night.

''I guess I should thank you.'' Her happiness with

the news made it easier for Rebecca to remove most of the resentment from her voice, but Josh heard what remained.

"The project merited the money," he insisted. "I didn't have anything to do with it."

"Bitsy!" Two voices now called her.

"What if we just stayed out here and didn't answer?" Josh wondered.

"Eventually they'd probably stir themselves enough to come searching for us."

"That's what I was afraid you'd say."

They followed the line of cornstalks back to the end of the field, hidden by the dark shadows and not bothering to answer Lauren's repeated shouts. By the time they reached the grassy lawn, Lauren had moved to the far side of the house and was calling down the road.

"Thank you for saying you didn't have anything to do with the funding," Rebecca called back to him as they moved through the field. If he answered, she couldn't hear him. She assumed Josh followed her all the way to the house, and it wasn't until she reached Lauren's side that she realized he had slipped away.

"Bitsy, where's Josh?"

"Oh." Rebecca smiled as she saw his headlights come on halfway down the drive. "I guess he went on home."

"Well! The least you could have done was invite him in for a while," Lauren chastised her irritably. "We drove all the way out here to see him, and you chased him off before we even had a chance to say hello. When are you ever going to learn how to entertain people?"

Rebecca followed her sister back into the house, her

smile lingering—not exactly polite, not exactly joyful, more like she had a private joke sending little bubbles of humor to the surface of her face. Long after everyone went home, Rebecca felt that smile returning to her lips with the memory of Josh grabbing her hand; but a familiar, cold fear kept chasing the smile away.

Chapter Four

"We'll just have to dig out the whole thing and then put the dirt back where you want it!" Tom Schwartz shouted over the caterwauling engine of the backhoe. "If we try to dig around, it's going to take longer, and it still might not be the way you want it!"

"Just make sure the islands are high enough!" Josh shouted back. "They can't be covered even when the water level is at its highest, so I want them three feet above the pond sides." He had insisted on raising three earthen nesting islands for the Canadian geese that would surely flock to the ponds that Rebecca was creating, but Rebecca had also insisted that he agree to three floating nest structures. The canoelike platforms would hold boxes built by her students and remain anchored even in high winds, and if the structures were available by the spring thaw, the geese would accept them as easily as the islands. Josh

50

wanted the naturalistic look of the islands, but Rebecca wanted another management activity for her students.

Rebecca hurried over before Tom took off again into the expanding depression. "I've marked the spot for the drainage pipe between the ponds, and another for the outlet to the creek. You need to make certain it's the right depth there. And the wheelchair ramps need to be a steady two to two-and-a-half feet below ground level and at least three feet wide. That's three feet after we shore up the dirt with the railroad ties, so the paths will have to be dug even wider."

"Yes, ma'am." Tom grinned and saluted lazily, then he reversed the backhoe into the pit, once more effectively ending any attempts at conversation.

Josh motioned her to follow him, and they moved away from the embryonic ponds and back to the area that had become a parking lot. With the introduction of heavy equipment, Josh had admitted the need for a graveled parking area, but each centimeter of cut land felt as if it were being sliced out of his own body. On the day Tom began digging out the ponds, Josh almost refused to watch, but Rebecca convinced him he was needed to help supervise the work.

"It's not so bad, is it?" she asked him, reaching for a thermos of coffee in her van. "Here. Have a cup."

Josh drank in silence, not answering her question.

"We're lucky the weather is holding. Even though it's cold, if we can get this dug out before the winter rains start, we'll be nearly a season ahead of my original schedule."

He nodded, staring back at Tom's steady chugging through the muddy hole.

"Come on, Josh. Are you going to whine every step of the way here? We're not hurting the land, we're going to manage it. We've got to take some risks if we want to make a future for this place.''

Finally he smiled at her. ''You're probably right. I know. I just hate seeing it so scarred. It's like we're digging the foundation for an apartment complex instead of ponds.'' He tried to convince himself he was making sound ecological decisions here, but he constantly worried that he would let things go too far just to keep her happy. He dreaded the thought that the day might come when he would be forced to overrule her.

''You've got to have some faith.'' She tossed out the dregs of her coffee and set the cup back in the van. ''Those muskrat dens will probably be back before Tom finishes his digging, and we're going to save that entire stand of cottonwoods. Want to come with me to start my inventory?''

''I'd like to, but I have to get back to my own work. I'm still managing the other two sites, and I need to evaluate those animal populations if I'm going to have a control for the effects here.''

Rebecca sighed and pulled out her clipboard and camera. ''Don't assume there will be problems before there actually are.''

''I shall do my best to remain objective, Ms. Traynor.'' He gave her his most scholarly raised eyebrow, and she giggled at the effect.

''Yeah, right. Go on and count your bugs, Dr. Mason. I'm going to go and count my bushes.''

''Maybe we could get together for dinner after we both finish all this sophisticated math. We could bring our calculators and tally up our results over Chinese food.'' He spoke as he wiped out his cup without looking at her.

"I . . . I'd like to," she stammered with an unexpected panic. "But . . . but I have to pick up Patty. I'm in charge for one more day, with Mom in D.C." All morning they had worked together with the comfortable familiarity of old times, a smooth team that understood each other almost intuitively. Now, with no warning, the atmosphere had changed to one of awkwardness and uncertainty.

"What about later?"

"I can't."

Josh waited for some explanation, but none came. "You know, Rebecca, it's all right for you to say you don't want to. I'm not trying to hassle you; I just wanted to have dinner with an old friend."

"I do want to!" She realized this came out with too much enthusiasm, and she tried to backtrack. "I mean . . . I would like to have dinner with you, but I just have too many responsibilities at home right now."

"So how about if I pick up Chinese for everybody, and bring it to your house? Is it just your dad and Patty again?"

"No. I mean, yes, it's just us. But no, you don't need to do that. Thanks anyway."

He heard it again: that light, airy voice that he hated so much. "Rebecca, don't do that."

"Do what?"

"Don't give me the polite talk. If you really don't want to have dinner with me, just say so. If you do, then just say that. I want to have dinner with you, and if that includes your dad and your niece, then that's okay, too." The look he gave her reminded her of the time she wouldn't admit that she didn't know how to use his fancy camera. Eventually he taught her, but he forced her to confess her ignorance first. "Just tell me what you want."

Rebecca took a deep breath, pulled the clipboard closer to her chest, and bit her lip. "All right. I'd like it. But I do have to stay at home. Dad won't handle Patty by himself. If you can put up with her, then I'd love to have you. But don't bring Chinese. I'm the only one who likes it. I'll fix something everybody will eat."

"Thank you." He backed away toward his truck. "I'll come over after I finish at Grove Marsh."

"It won't be fancy!" she shouted after him as he pulled out of the lot.

"Who cares?" he called back.

"Who cares?" Rebecca argued as they sat at the large dining room table after dinner. "If density counts are time-consuming, then it's my time that's being consumed. I think that the best way to measure the health of the vegetation is to count individual plants within each unit." She shoved a development map across the table toward Josh. "I already have abundance ratings on six species in the woods to the north of the second pond."

Josh glanced at the brightly colored cross-hatching on the map and shook his head. "But measuring cover rather than density would be a lot more helpful."

"Why? I need to know what's there, so that I can control the excess growth and get the maximum variety of plants. A density count will be the most accurate."

Josh sighed and turned the map back toward Rebecca. "What's the purpose of all those latest plants, Rebecca? This isn't just some garden you're planting so the ladies' club can sit there and look at flowers while they drink their tea.''

"Tea!" Patty's interruption warded off Rebecca's sharp reply. "Tea!"

"Do you like flowers?" Josh asked the little girl, willing to be diverted from the argument for a few minutes.

"Tea! Tea! Tea!" Patty sang the words without looking at Josh, and he thought she had ignored him until she insisted, "Flowers!"

"Do you want me to look at your flowers, Patty?" he asked.

Patty stood and walked to the kitchen door that opened onto the kitchen garden Rebecca had planted. The last of the year's mums staunchly braved the chilly days and cold nights, their tips showing the lightest kisses of frosted brown. "Tea-Flowers."

He laughed and reached out to ruffle her hair.

"No! *No!* NO!" Patty shouted in that disconcerting voice, her volume increasing even as her inflection flattened to a total lack of expression.

Josh jerked his hand back quickly and stepped away from her. "I'm sorry, Patty. I'm sor—"

"Patty, it's all right," Rebecca interrupted. "It's all right. Look at the flowers. Let's pick one for Grandpa. Pick a flower for Grandpa."

"Flower-Grandpa."

Josh watched as Rebecca held one flower after another, letting Patty pull them off by the heads or by the roots until the child had a handful of decimated petals and leaves.

"Take these to Grandpa, Patty," Rebecca ordered, and the little girl mechanically walked off to the living room. "He won't appreciate them, but at least he won't yell at her."

"Why would anyone yell at her?" Josh asked. "She's so innocent."

Rebecca stared at him for a minute and then returned to the table and their map. She wanted to rush back to the argument about her methodology, but her eyes felt hot with tears.

"Rebecca?" She looked up to see his quiet, troubled face.

"People don't understand. They think she does the things she does because she's bad. They think she could control herself if someone just disciplined her better. It's always difficult when someone doesn't understand why she acts the way she does."

She waited for the inevitable stupid comments about how Patty would probably grow out of this, about how therapy would help, about how Patty should be in an institution where she could be trained properly, or even about how she seemed like a normal kid, but Josh didn't make any of those comments. Instead he covered her hand with his own and said, "That makes it hard on her family, I bet."

"Yeah, well . . ." Rebecca hesitated in confusion. "Let's get back to the vegetation measurement."

"Plants are a lot easier, aren't they? They never talk back to you." He laughed, and Rebecca felt her skin flush from her forehead down to her shoulders at the truth of his words.

"So tell me again what's wrong with density measures?" she groused.

"We need to relate the plant life to the general ecology of the site," he insisted. "If you measure how much basal area covers the ground, we'll have some notion of how hospitable each area is to wildlife, and we can compare the various habitats with the same dimension.''

''But that doesn't tell me much about the plants, and how I need to design my schedule for tending them.''

''But the purpose of all those plants is to provide habitat for the animals.''

''But the purpose of my grant is to provide horticultural therapy for my students!''

''Bitsy!'' Patty entered the dining room again, still carrying her bits and pieces of flowers. ''Bit . . . sy!'' The child's wide-open yawn interrupted her call.

''All right, Patty. Let's get you ready for bed.'' At Patty's automatic stiffening of resistance, Rebecca shrugged at Josh. ''Sorry. I should have warned you we wouldn't have much chance to discuss work.''

''Don't worry about it. Go on and put her to bed. I'll just go see your dad for a few minutes.''

''Oh. Okay.'' She assumed he would be gone by the time she managed to quiet her niece for the night, and she heard herself switch on what he called ''the voice'' as she added, ''Well, I'll see you, then.''

Nearly an hour later, wet from Patty's bathwater and frazzled from the last fifteen minutes of Patty's agitation, Rebecca trudged back downstairs to clean up the kitchen. Her father sat contentedly in the living room, watching television and reading the Farm Bureau newsletter at the same time. She couldn't begrudge him his peace and quiet at night, since she knew he worked relentlessly all day, but she would have appreciated some help with the dishes after her own long day. With a sigh she walked back to the kitchen.

Josh stood at the sink with his back to her, drying the broiling pan and setting it carefully next to the other clean dishes. She must have made a sound, because he turned around and grinned at her.

"I didn't know where these things went, or I would have put them away. My mom always says that a stranger in the kitchen is more trouble than he's worth."

"I . . ." She couldn't think of anything to say. Why did such a small kindness make her so nervous? "You didn't have to do this," she said gruffly, putting pans and lids away quickly in an effort to camouflage her emotion. Josh stood silently while she finished shelving the last of the plates and made a final crack about how guests shouldn't be expected to clean up after themselves.

"Rebecca."

"What?"

"Say 'thank you.' "

"Thank you." She couldn't look at him.

"You're welcome." As he spoke he reached out and encircled her wrist gently with his large, strong fingers, pulling her toward him ever so slightly.

"Hey, Bits! How about making some coffee?" her father called in from the living room, and Josh released her wrist with a sigh.

"Do you ever have any time when other people aren't asking you to do something?" he asked.

"Not often." She reached for the coffee filters and efficiently started the pot. "It comes from living with a large family."

"I understand that. But it always seemed to me that

they depend on you more than any of the others. You were always such a mother hen to everybody, even your older sisters. I'm sort of surprised you aren't married with a half dozen kids of your own by now.''

Rebecca reached into the cabinet and retrieved three mugs, opened the refrigerator for the milk, and finally found a spoon for the sugar bowl, but she didn't respond to his statement. She delicately removed the lid from the sugar bowl and placed it on the counter with the precision of an artist.

''Rebecca?'' Josh knew the signs.

''What?'' she snapped, letting a shadow of her irritability show.

''I didn't mean to make you mad.''

She pulled the pot away from the coffeemaker before it had finished dripping, and brown liquid splashed onto the hot plate and over the kitchen counter. ''Rats,'' she mumbled, shoving the offending pot back in its spot.

''Rebecca?'' He leaned close and spoke very softly. ''That was intended as a compliment, not an insult.''

Rebecca lifted her eyes from the nearly finished coffee, searched his face carefully, and twitched her fingers as if she wanted to reach up and touch something. Reluctantly Josh forced himself to move away from her. His father's old warnings blared like trumpets in his head. *''You're too old for this girl. You'll put too much pressure on her. It isn't fair to take advantage of a child who looks up to you the way Rebecca looks up to you.''*

''I really don't think I want to talk about this,'' she finally answered, a hauntingly familiar disappointment settling on her. ''It's not any of your business, anyway.''

"You're right. It's none of my business." He backed away another step and waited for her to finish the coffee.

They sat in the living room with her father, and Josh watched in amazement as Bob gulped the scalding liquid in three quick swallows.

"Thanks, Bitsy. I'll say good night now." Bob shook hands quickly with Josh and disappeared up the stairs.

With a bemused frown, Rebecca watched her father go. "Oh, well, I guess he didn't want to listen to us talk about plant cover."

"I think he may just be giving a subtle hint that it's time for me to leave," Josh said, setting down his own coffee cup. "We can finish this at work." He left the way he had always left: hands shoved deep in his pockets, head tossed quickly back in a boy's noncommittal farewell gesture, and a brief "See ya!" The routine insured that he never put his hands on her.

At the top of the stairs, Bob Traynor shook his head in disgust, rolled his eyes, and wondered what the younger generation was coming to.

After Josh agreed to allow Rebecca to pour concrete to hold several raised beds for her plants, she compromised and redrew her plan according to the basal cover provided by the various species. She sympathized with his concern over the loss of cover due to the construction work, and she wanted to help out his animal and bird populations as much as possible. Trying to keep the terrain wild, but accessible to her students, was proving to be more difficult than she had first thought.

The class made their first field trip to the marsh long before the grounds were truly wheelchair accessible, but Josh found a few Parks and Rec volunteers who worked with the students for their first experiment. The students collected several different types of soil from the area, which they took back to their classroom to test for drainage, ability to hold water, and acidity. They would then begin their own research on the best native plants for the area.

The ponds weren't yet filled, the brush that had been cut down had not yet been hauled away, and the students wound up muddy and tired, but everyone proclaimed the experience a resounding success. Most of these students rarely had the opportunity to dig in the dirt, and none of them had ever contributed their own physical labor to protect a wilderness. Rebecca could feel their enthusiasm growing even when their wheels and walkers became entrenched in the mud and had to be dug out by the volunteers.

Several deer skittered away from the field when the noisy students first arrived, but two fattening groundhogs waddled unconcernedly at the edge of the tall grass throughout the morning. A flock of migrating robins filled several hawthorn trees near the edge of the woods, and a vee of geese glided vociferously toward their itinerant home in the nearby reservoir. As the students dug their samples, they exclaimed over the number of insects still moving around this late in the year.

The classroom teacher, Cindy White, couldn't praise Rebecca enough. ''For years I've been trying to get the school board to offer some of these nontraditional services for my students, but they complain about the cost and doubt the benefits. If they could only see what we've seen today!''

Listening to the students arguing about the value of

putting a trail through the woods or leaving it natural, Rebecca realized that these young people had already taken ownership of the park. Whatever happened, these students now belonged here and had a sense of responsibility for the outcome of this project. They would never again passively observe a living, growing landscape without understanding some of the power of cultivation, without remembering the satisfaction of holding rich damp soil in their hands. And they would also know the importance of the foliage to the animal life it sustains.

"You were right about this project," Josh congratulated her as the last of the school vans pulled out of the graveled lot.

"So were you," Rebecca admitted a little sheepishly.

"What do you mean?"

"There is more to this than just making a beautiful place. I know that the aesthetics are important, but the fact is, we're providing habitat. Maybe we're even providing habitat for these kids."

"I knew I could talk you around to my way of thinking. You always were a pushover for helpless creatures."

"I am not!" she objected, indignant with the image. "I'm not a pushover at all."

"Just for the helpless, Rebecca. I'd choose you as a guerilla warrior against the bullies anytime." Josh grinned at her with the same grin he had used the afternoon they wreaked vengeance on some of Josh's less-sensitive classmates. "Do you remember the revenge of the birds?"

The summer after he graduated, he had taken

Rebecca with him on a long hike through Delaware State Park, and they had slipped quietly past a beer party being held near the campgrounds. Both had just rolled their eyes and kept going, but later they returned by the same route. Plastic rings from the six-packs littered the ground along with plastic bags and a sizable amount of cast-off food. Already animals had consumed some of the plastic in their efforts to get at the leftovers.

Josh and Rebecca had cleaned up the mess and left, but he came back by her house after dark and let her ride with him to carry out his plan of retribution. Three of the boys had received cars as graduation presents. The next morning all three of them discovered that the paint on their new cars had been devastated by bird droppings and small scratches. None of them ever noticed the birdseed that had been generously scattered on their vehicles as an early morning feast for the feathered vandals.

"That was one of our best, wasn't it?" she asked with a laugh.

"I've always thought so. We made a great team."

Standing now in the last of the autumn sun, enjoying the clearest skies of the year and the musky smell of decaying leaves swirling around them, Rebecca could nearly forget the intervening years and pretend they were still the two friends who had had so much fun during her childhood. Others may have considered their partnership odd—her sisters certainly had teased her about following Josh around like a puppy—but she and Josh blended comfortably together from the beginning. With a little shake of her head, Rebecca pulled herself back to the present. She wasn't a child any longer, and she understood that Josh Mason had simply been a very nice boy who had tolerated her hero-worship until he moved on to more important things.

Chapter Five

As Rebecca turned off Route 23 and headed down the little county road toward home, she heaved a sigh of relief. Friday-afternoon traffic on the highway exhausted her, and she berated herself for not making her trip to Big Island Nature Preserve during the middle of the week. At least she had succeeded in finding plenty of material for seeding her pond banks, and she made a mental note to thank the naturalist at the preserve for letting her wander among the marshes for dried seeds.

The driveway to the farmhouse overflowed with cars and trucks when she finally reached it, and Rebecca drove over the grass to reach her own parking spot back by the barn. By the time she had double-checked the bags of seeds and locked her van, a swarm of young boys came racing across the yard to jump on her.

"Bitsy! Aunt Bitsy!" She nearly fell down with the onslaught of laughing, excited children. "We get to stay for the whole weekend! Can we go see the cows?"

"Grandpa said you would teach us to drive the tractor! But not Danny, he's too little."

"I think Robbie's too little, too. Not me. I'm in kindergarten now."

"Let's see cows! Bitsy! Bitsy!"

"I am not too little to drive the tractor, Micky. Grandpa said!"

Before the hostilities could become violent, Rebecca scooped up the three-year-old Danny, placed him on her hip, and started marching toward the house. "Come on, you guys. Grandpa started this, Grandpa can finish it. If he wants you to drive the tractor, he can just teach you himself." She wouldn't take her frustration out on her three nephews, but she certainly didn't intend to allow her father to rope her into putting three small boys on the tractor.

Denise and Mike stood poised beside their minivan, Denise holding the car seat that she still insisted Danny use. Rebecca wondered if Denise had heard of the tractor-driving plan.

"Hi, Bitsy," Mike greeted her. "It's really nice of you to watch the kids for us this weekend."

"Let's go, Mike," Denise urged, shoving the car seat in Rebecca's direction. "The traffic is so bad we'll never get to the concert on time."

Rebecca reached for the car seat without thinking. "Where are you going?"

"Tonight we're going to a concert at the Polaris, and tomorrow we have tickets to the BalletMet in town. We figured it would just be easier to leave the kids here for the whole weekend than to try to drive back and forth so many times." Denise had enough conscience to look a little sheepish, but she refused to acknowledge that she might be taking advantage of her sister. "Dad said it would be all right."

"I'm sure he did," Rebecca answered. "I'm sure Dad won't mind at all." She wondered why this happened so many times, but she couldn't imagine any way to prevent it. "In fact, I understand that Mom and Dad are going to Indianapolis tomorrow morning for the Farm Show. I heard them say they were going to spend the night."

Denise was already in the car, but Mike stood by his door looking at Rebecca in confusion. "Is something wrong?" he asked. "Are you not going to be able to watch the kids?" He seemed truly befuddled by Rebecca's comments and he began to show signs of panic that his plans would be foiled. As always, Rebecca couldn't stand the thought of hurting anyone's feelings, and she knew she would regret it if she refused to help her sister.

"No. Of course not. Nothing's wrong." She smiled, listening to her voice lift in what Josh called her "polite talk." "I just didn't know all the plans." Rebecca leaned down to force her sister to answer her. "You really don't expect me to let the boys start driving the tractor this weekend, do you?"

With a look of horror, Denise screamed, "No! Absolutely not! What are you thinking of, Bitsy? Don't you dare let them get around the farm equipment!"

The older two boys groaned in disappointment, but Danny seemed interested only in getting to the cows. With some satisfaction that she could blame at least one "no" on their mother, Rebecca resigned herself to another weekend of full-time child care for her nephews and scooted them into the farmhouse. At least her two youngest sisters would be home to help watch the boys.

Chaos met her with its usual noisy burst as she stepped into the house. Caitlin bounded down the stairs three at a time, trailing a skirt and blouse over her head like a wind-whipped banner. "I get to use the iron first, Lindsey!" she shouted to the sister following on her heels. "Johnny is picking me up first."

"I don't care. I'll get the hot water first." Lindsey laughed as she turned around and retreated up the steps. "And I'll take my time drying my hair, too!"

Rebecca dropped Danny on his feet in the hallway and he immediately grabbed onto her hand. "I'm hungry, Aunt Bitsy. I want my dinner."

"Come on, sport, and let's see what Grandma has fixed for you," Rebecca replied optimistically. She pulled him down the hallway into the kitchen just in time to see her mother hand the iron to Caitlin. For once, nothing delicious simmered on the stove.

"I'm all finished, honey," she said as she carefully folded a dress into her suitcase and snapped the lid closed with a satisfied flourish. "We'll be out of everyone's way in five minutes."

Rebecca felt her heart sink. "Mom?"

"Oh, there you are, Bits. I was beginning to think you might not make it home on time. Your head gets more scatterbrained every day." Mrs. Traynor shoved her suitcase out of the kitchen toward the front door. "I told you we were going to leave by six, and it's already six-fifteen."

"Mom, you told me you were going to leave tomorrow morning at six."

Her mother shook her head but avoided Rebecca's eyes. "No, I'm sure I told you . . . oh, maybe that was Denise I told. I'm sure I told one of you, anyway. . . . Well, no harm done. You're here and we're ready to go. We'll be back Sunday evening. Don't worry about the cows. Mr. Martin promised to keep an eye on them."

Danny pulled on her hand again. "Aunt Bitsy, I'm hungry!"

"Just a minute, Danny," she answered, trying to keep calm. "Mom, you didn't tell me that Denise wanted me to watch the boys this weekend."

"I didn't?" Faye asked as Bob helped her into her coat. "I thought I had. Didn't I, Bob?"

"Well, it won't matter too much," Bob replied. "After all, Colleen came to pick up Patty this afternoon, so you wouldn't have anything to do this weekend anyway."

Before Rebecca could answer, Faye added, "And I arranged for Lindsey and Caitlin to stay in town with the Mortons after the football game. That way you won't have to worry about waiting up for them or getting them to the library tomorrow. All you have to do is keep an eye on the boys." She turned to her husband. "Thank you, dear. I'm all ready now." She flushed with excitement and smiled as if she were a young girl leaving for a first date.

The smoldering heat of anger and frustration died before it could fan into flames of temper beneath Rebecca's calm exterior, and she knew she couldn't say anything that would ruin her mother's weekend. Both of her parents worked so hard to take care of this family, Rebecca could at least pull her share of the load to help out her sisters. She swallowed hard to cover any remnants of resentment and kissed her parents on the cheek.

"Have a good time," she said, smiling weakly. "I'll see you Sunday."

"Aunt Bitsy! I'm hungry!" Little Danny wouldn't wait patiently any longer, and Rebecca knew that Micky and Robbie would start complaining soon.

"Okay. Let's go see if I can find some hot dogs for you." While Lindsey and Caitlin rushed past each other primping for their dates, Rebecca managed to find a package of frozen hot dogs, a can of corn, and a basket of Red Rome apples for the children. The boys were quietly sitting at the table eating when the two teenagers left for the game, and Rebecca finally had a chance to collapse in a chair in the living room. She couldn't bear the thought of eating hot dogs, and she hadn't had any appetite since she reached home, anyway.

It had started out as such a perfect day, too. She had wandered up and down the dikes at Big Island, shaking seeds into her bags, pulling out her guidebooks to identify some of the more subtle differences in the sedges and rushes. Except for the naturalist who had met her briefly when she arrived, Rebecca had not seen another soul for the entire day and she had reveled in the solitude. She even allowed herself to enjoy the animal life, watching the huge population of Canadian geese suddenly lifting en masse when something startled them. To her delight, the culprit was a lone red fox who slunk out of the underbrush practically at her feet, took one look at her, and disappeared without a trace.

"I should take lessons from that fox on how to avoid unwanted company," she murmured to herself as the boys finished their dinner and tumbled over one another like puppies on their way to the television set. Lifting herself from the chair, she headed toward the kitchen and the stack of dishes yet to be done. She was only half finished when the phone rang.

"Micky, would you get that for me? My hands are soapy," she called. She heard the thudding of feet as Robbie tried to beat his brother to the phone, but the ringing stopped before anyone crashed and screamed so she assumed they managed to settle on a winner without bloodshed. She turned her attention back to the dishes, assuming some window replacement salesman could enjoy the pleasure of her nephew's conversation for a few minutes, and by the time she left the kitchen she had forgotten all about the phone call.

"All right, Danny. You get your bath first this evening," she declared. "Let's go." She actually enjoyed taking care of the boys. The three of them combined could be managed about as easily as Patty alone, and at least they communicated their own needs well. Not only that, but unlike Patty, they expressed their love for her with constant hugs and kisses, and Rebecca sometimes wondered what she would do without this one haven of affection.

Micky's bath came last, and his six-year-old's modesty demanded that she remain outside the bathroom, but she stood a close sentinel, shouting exhortations through the door for him to be sure to use soap. She had just decided that he had been in long enough to soak clean when she heard someone at the front door.

"Hurry and get out, Micky. There's someone at the door." She shouted to Robbie, "Don't open the door until I get there!" But the boys all started yelling at once.

"It's okay. It's just that guy on the phone!"

"It's the guy with the food!"

Micky ran out of the bathroom with a towel partially wrapped around his waist. "It's your boyfriend, Aunt Bitsy. He said he'd bring us pizza! Hurry up!"

"What are you talking about?" Rebecca shouted, following his trail of water down the stairs. "You go back upstairs and dry off and put your pajamas on, Micky!"

By this time, Robbie had the front door opened and was pulling Josh Mason, arms loaded with bags and boxes, into the hallway. Rebecca stopped halfway down the steps and stared. Josh handed a large red-and-white pizza box to Micky, who immediately ran into the living room with it, nearly losing his towel as he ran.

"Oh boy, pepperoni!"

Josh grinned at Rebecca and held up two plain brown paper bags. "Don't worry. I brought us Chinese."

"What are you doing here?" she asked, unable to continue her descent.

"Didn't anybody tell you?"

"Who? What?"

"I called this afternoon, and your dad said I should call back around seven. When I called back I got your personal answering service."

Rebecca raised a skeptical eyebrow.

"The boys," he explained. "They invited me to come over. They informed me that, unbelievable as it may be, you don't like hot dogs, and you hadn't eaten. I offered to bring you some real food, and they accepted on your behalf as long as I also brought them a pizza."

Rebecca remained rooted where she stood, the sudden fluttering in her stomach vacillating between excitement and panic. She felt thickheaded, as if she couldn't quite comprehend what brought Josh here with a pizza for her nephews, and she alternated between the pleasure of seeing him and irritation at one more unexpected turn in the day's events. He watched her curiously for a few minutes, then shrugged and grinned.

"If you don't want to eat, you don't have to," he joked, "but it's hot-and-sour soup, and chicken with mushrooms. I know you love it, but you don't have to eat it. Anyway, come and talk to me while I eat. Tell me about your day at Big Island."

Finally she was jolted into action, and she ran the last few steps to grab the bag out of his hand.

"There is no way I am going to sit there and watch you make a pig of yourself with all this food, Josh Mason. I'm going to have to help you restrain yourself by having my share." She led the way back into the kitchen, shouting once more to Micky to put on his pajamas and futilely reminding the boys to use napkins.

An hour later she sent Josh in to keep the boys company while she made coffee. While it dripped she finished the last of the cleanup, then she poured a cup for Josh and carried it into the living room for him to drink while she put the boys to bed. To her surprise, the living room stood clean and empty. A few muffled giggles echoed down the stairs just before she heard Josh say firmly, "But that's only if I don't have to come back up here to get you quiet." Then his footsteps sounded easily on the steps and he came smiling into the living room.

"Ah, you angel. Coffee is a wonderful idea. Can I have a cup, too?" He started back toward the kitchen.

"No. I mean, this is for you." Rebecca held out the cup just as the door opened and Colleen stomped into the house dragging a passively resistant Patty by one wrist.

The child kept her head down and emitted a low-pitched, steady moan while her free hand flailed around her head. Colleen appeared nearly distraught as she plowed into the living room with her daughter. Rebecca's arm stretched toward Josh with the cup of hot coffee, Josh backed away when Patty nearly collided with him, and suddenly Patty's swinging hand knocked the coffee into a flying arch that landed on her with a ferocious, scalding splat.

Patty's moan soared into a hurt and angry scream. "Aahh! Aahh!" No words were needed for her to express her protest.

Colleen dropped her daughter's hand and tried to put her arms around her in comfort, but Patty screamed louder and stood with the rigidity of steel. She shook her head so hard that she hit Colleen's jaw with a resounding thud, and Colleen added her own howl to the noise as she backed away.

"Stop it, Patty!" Colleen shouted. "Just stop it!" Tears flowed from her eyes and she started to reach for her daughter again until Rebecca stepped in front of her.

"Slow down, Colleen," Rebecca urged quietly. "She'll just get worse." Rebecca reached for her sister's hands and held them clasped tightly in her own. "It will be all right. Just slow down."

Out of the corner of her eye, Rebecca watched Josh slip quickly into the kitchen, leaving Patty to form her own protective cocoon of sound and motion. Pulling Colleen into a hug, Rebecca soothed her sister the way Colleen had tried to soothe her daughter, stroking her back and crooning softly that everything would be all right. The anger and frustration drained out of Colleen's muscles, and in their place Rebecca could feel the heaving release of desperate sobbing.

Eventually, Colleen's tears slowed to hiccups as Patty's screams descended into monotonous moaning and her violent shaking became a steady, rhythmical rocking. Rebecca pulled away from Colleen to find Josh kneeling beside Patty and holding an ice pack gently against her burnt arm. He carefully refrained from touching her in any other way. The three boys peered through the banister watching the entire scene, but they apparently knew better than to come too close to the fray.

"I can't do this," Colleen spoke with the flat, dead voice of utter defeat. "I know I can't keep taking advantage of you, Bitsy, but I just can't do this."

Rebecca patted her back again. "Yes, you can, Colleen. You just need to slow down with her."

Colleen glanced at her stiffly rocking daughter, sighed heavily, and shook her head. "No. I can't." She focused on Rebecca, a flash of anger spicing her sadness. "I just can't do it anymore. I'm going to have Chuck call that home in Cambridge."

Rebecca dropped her arms to her sides in shock. "What? Colleen, you can't mean that."

"Bitsy, I'm going home. You'll have to keep her for me tonight. I'm afraid of what I might do if I try to take her back home with me. We may have to wait until after the weekend, but I'm going to see to it that she gets into an institution where she belongs." Colleen turned on her heel and stalked out the door, leaving behind the shock of her three nephews, her sister, and her sister's friend. Her daughter simply stared at the floor, rocking and moaning, rocking and moaning, lost in a world inaccessible to any of them.

Chapter Six

The agitated whip of the old rocking chair gradually eased to a gentler swing and finally slowed to a stop as Patty worked out of her tension and eventually fell asleep. Josh joined Rebecca on the sofa after putting the boys back to bed and calming their fears about Patty and Colleen.

"Are they okay?" Rebecca asked softly.

"They didn't understand what was happening, and Danny was afraid that his mom might decide to send him away to a home if he screamed too much." Josh rested his elbows on his knees and stared sadly at Patty's sleeping form. "It's hard, isn't it?"

Rebecca nodded. "I don't know what to do for Colleen. After Patty was born, she tried so hard to give her the love and nurturing a normal baby needs, and poor Patty would lie in her arms, stiff as a board. When Colleen realized that it was a neurological prob-

77

lem, she and Chuck went from doctor to doctor, trying to find a cure. Finally they realized that they couldn't 'fix' her and Colleen sort of went crazy. She was so terrified of having another autistic child.'' Rebecca closed her eyes for a few seconds at the painful memory. ''Then when Ashley was born and was obviously normal and healthy, Colleen practically gave up trying to be a mother to Patty.''

Josh nodded but didn't take his eyes off the child. ''So you took over the job?''

Rebecca shrugged. ''Over the past three years I've had Patty with me more and more. I think it's easier because I'm not her mother. I don't grieve because she never hugs me. I don't blame myself because she can't look me in the eye. I don't think it's my personal failure that her speech is so behind. Colleen does all those things.''

She waited for the blame and criticism to come, the easy expectation that the right solution could be found for this complex situation. Instead Josh stood quietly and gestured with his head toward Patty's frail body.

''Is she sound asleep now? I'll carry her to bed for you.''

''There's no need. I can take her up.'' Rebecca rose and Josh touched her arm.

''I know you can. I know I don't need to do this. Can't you let me help?''

''You've already done so much tonight.'' Her protest came automatically. ''This can't have been much fun for you, coming out here to help me baby-sit my monster nephews and ending up in the middle of a family catastrophe.''

Josh grinned. ''Actually, I kind of liked most of it. Your monster nephews are a hoot. In fact, I suggested

to them that they might like to come out to the barn
with us tomorrow and sort those seeds you collected
today.''

"You didn't!''

"Sure I did. And if Patty is doing better, she could
come too, couldn't she?''

"Well . . .''

"I know . . . we'll see. That's a favorite line for
moms and bossy aunts to use.'' He leaned over the
rocking chair and lifted Patty. Even in deep sleep, the
child didn't nestle close to him but remained somewhat stiff and unresponsive to his careful embrace.
"Show me where she sleeps.''

They climbed the stairs and followed the long hallway of the large house, and Rebecca pointed to the
low trundle bed in the corner of her own room. Josh
laid Patty down and then let his eyes roam around the
fresh, neat room while Rebecca managed to dress the
sleeping girl in a clean nightgown. The multitude of
hanging, climbing, and blooming plants didn't particularly surprise Josh, but the tightly packed bookcases
did. He read a few titles, recognizing a number of texts
on wildlife management and wetland ecology, and
whistled over several books on autism and neuropsy-
chology. Moving on to the other shelves he found
books on educational theory, Alzheimer's disease, the
management of family farms, horticultural therapy,
and half a dozen Peterson guides to various types of
wildlife, but he didn't see any fiction at all. He wondered if she still read poetry.

"She's settled now.'' Rebecca spoke softly from the
doorway where she watched Josh finish his survey of
her room.

"Don't you ever read novels anymore?'' he asked,

grinning a little and following her out of the dimly lit room. "I seem to remember one summer when you swore to read every classic ever written."

Rebecca shrugged. "I was young and naive back then."

The bitterness came through so sharply that Josh felt an actual pain in his chest. What had happened to his lovely, happy child-friend that had turned her into this cautious, controlled young woman? Did Patty's care demand so much self-control that Rebecca no longer allowed herself to experience life's emotions? He watched her walk ahead of him, the glow from the hallway lamp turning her thick, dark hair into a glowing mass of deep auburn, reminding him of a time years ago when she had stood in a similar glow in his parents' garage.

"Do you remember the quail chicks?" he asked.

"Of course I do!" She spun around and temporarily cast aside all his concerns with her flashing smile. "I could never forget them."

A farmer's dog had managed to kill both of the parent quails before Josh could stop it, but Rebecca had found the clutch of tiny eggs and scooped them into her baseball cap while Josh chased the dog away. It was the last summer he had spent with her, before his father warned him off, and the two had put in long hours incubating the eggs and hatching the chicks. One of the eggs never hatched, and three of the chicks died, but eight furry balls survived and grew and eventually flew away. Josh had recorded the entire project for one of his professors, who raved about the success. Rebecca had cried over each failed baby and claimed that a seventy-five-percent success rate was barely passing.

Now, standing in the upstairs hallway listening to the sleeping sounds of her niece and nephews, Josh watched Rebecca remember the magical feelings of that summer when they had worked together to save something precious and fragile. He could practically see the images going through her mind as she remembered the excitement of cracking shells, the anxiety of tiny fledglings following her out of the garage and into the yard for their first walk, and the bittersweet relief when they flew away to face the dangers of Farmer Miller's dog. Patty moaned softly in her sleep, bringing their thoughts back to the present.

"You've always been great with animals and small children," Josh praised her.

"I'm still only managing a seventy-five-percent success rate." She grimaced, glancing back toward Patty's room.

"I thought you said you didn't feel guilty about Patty."

"I feel guilty about Colleen. And I just know I do better with plants." She resumed the climb back downstairs and halted at the bottom by the front door. "Thanks for helping out tonight. I'm sorry I sounded so ungrateful earlier. I guess I'm not used to letting anybody else help out."

"It's all right. I really did have a good time, and I'll be back in the morning to help with the seeds. What time do you think the monsters will get up?"

She laughed ruefully. "Probably before seven, but I can hold them down with the TV set at least until nine."

"I'll see you around then."

"Josh, you really don't have to do this. The seeds are my responsibility and I'm used to taking care of

the kids. I'm sure you have better things to do with
your weekend than hang around here.''

He sighed at her use of "the voice." "Why is it so
hard for you?''

"What?" she asked, but she knew what he meant.

"I've been your friend for most of our lives, but
you treat me as if I'm just some nosy neighbor offer-
ing to butt into your life. We always did things together before. We always helped each other out. That
was half the fun. Why is it so hard to do that now?''

Rebecca felt a sudden surge of anger she hadn't
known she still felt. How dare he blame her for the
strain on their relationship? Just as quickly she felt a
stab of fear and she shut off all of her feelings. Josh
watched her pull herself away from the companionable
warmth they had shared all evening, saw her wrap
herself in some icy protective shell and move to a
place where he couldn't reach her.

"Please, Rebecca. Why can't we be friends again?
Why won't you let me help out?''

He wanted her to explain it to him, but when she
spoke it was with that dreadful, disengaged voice. Not
angry, not hurt, just very polite.

"I'm used to handling things by myself. It's really
no problem.''

"Is it a problem to let me help?" He fixed her with
that look of his that demanded honesty.

"I don't want you to help me anymore . . . again.''
She would give him the answer he demanded, but she
would not let him see that she still felt the pain. "A
long time ago I thought you were my friend, Josh. I
trusted you more than I trusted anyone else in the
world. I depended on you . . . And you just disappeared when you got tired of me. I don't think I'll

ever let you do that to me again.'' She wanted to sound cold. She wanted him to see that she no longer cared about it, and she fought not to sound like that hurt, scared teenager from so long ago. She nearly succeeded.

But Josh listened with an ear that understood how she used her aloofness as a disguise of her true feelings. After all these years of nursing his own loss, he wondered for the first time if she also had grieved when their friendship ended. His father had thoroughly convinced him that sixteen-year-old Rebecca Traynor neither needed nor wanted some college boy hanging around. According to his parents, even Rebecca's sisters thought his interest in her was weird, and he assumed Rebecca experienced nothing more than some mild relief when he left for school and didn't return.

''I didn't know you felt that way,'' he stated quietly. ''I . . . had to go away,'' he stammered, unsure of how much to explain. ''Do you understand? You were only sixteen.''

''I understand completely,'' she replied, this time able to achieve the completely disinterested tone she wanted. ''I was only sixteen.'' *Only sixteen, and not worth your time or effort even to write a note explaining that you were moving away from me and outgrowing your little friend.* Oh, she could still feel the bitterness if she let herself, but she wouldn't let him know it. She had promised herself that when she started working on this project. She wouldn't dwell on the way he had disappointed her, but she also wouldn't give him the opportunity to do it again. ''I like working together, but I'm not sixteen anymore, and I can take care of my own life.''

"I know you can. In fact, you always could. I just enjoy doing things with you."

"Fine." She could hardly avoid him if she continued with her project.

"Fine." He breathed a sigh and tried to be glad that at least she hadn't banished him completely. "I'll see you in the morning." He grabbed his jacket off the back of a nearby chair and made a quick escape before she could suddenly change her mind and tell him not to come.

Leaning her head against the door, Rebecca calmed her heart rate with slow, even breaths and wondered how she could feel so frightened and so hopeful at the same time. How could she want him to leave her alone at the same time that she celebrated having him back in her life? She would just have to learn how to walk this particular emotional tightrope.

"Okay," she whispered to the night. "Fine."

Winter blew in overnight, and a frosty glaze crowned the stubble in the cornfield with a reflecting brightness. Rebecca enjoyed the view out the kitchen window while she washed the cereal bowls and took quick sips of her rapidly cooling coffee. The three boys half-heartedly pulled on their socks and boots, complaining that their aunt really should let them watch cartoons until noon and simultaneously telling her to hurry up so they could get to the barn. Patty sat at the computer desk, still operating a little under par after her difficult evening, but no longer screaming or flailing.

"All right, you guys, let's break out of this joint," Rebecca finally called to them. "Everybody get a jacket; it's going to be cold in the barn." Sorting the seeds into the various types would allow her to include identification skills in her learning objectives for the students who would work with her in the spring. She could also help them set up some experiments measuring the benefits of different planting and cultivation methods for different species. By spring, the boardwalks would be completed, the ponds would be filled, and the soil would be ready to receive these seeds.

After snapping Patty's jacket closed, Rebecca let her niece grab a finger and they followed the boys across the yard to the barn. When Josh hadn't shown up at the house by 9:15, Rebecca assumed he had thought better of the situation and decided to stay home after all, but when she reached the barn, she saw his truck pulled in alongside her van. The barn door stood partially opened, and the boys scrambled through the narrow opening, shouting with joy at the sight of their new friend.

"Hi, Josh!"

"What's that thing?"

"When did you get here?"

They all spoke at once and rushed to climb up his long legs in the rough-and-tumble exuberance of young males. Rebecca laughed and stood with Patty, watching Josh organize the boys without dampening their enthusiasm. He handled them with an impressive natural discipline, and she realized how much easier this task would be with his help than by herself. He had already pulled two sawhorses out of the corner of the barn and now directed the boys to help him lay a couple of long planks across them.

Rebecca dragged her large paper bag full of seeds into the middle of the barn, took one of the feed scoops off the wall, and spread a collection of her bounty onto the board.

"Here you go, boys," she said as she handed each of them a small pile of brown envelopes. "Each envelope should contain only one kind of seed. That means you have to sort them into piles of different kinds and then scrape the piles into separate envelopes."

They groaned a little, just for effect, and settled into a fairly efficient workforce. Even little Danny seemed able to distinguish between the various types of seeds, and Rebecca smiled at his efforts. She pulled up a barrel, sat down, and began her own work, half aware that Patty had gathered a pile of seeds to play with also. The girl's incessant rocking seemed to relax a little as she mumbled to herself and dragged the seeds into piles.

Josh worked at the far end of the makeshift table, keeping up a running monologue to the boys about why the seeds had their various shapes and sizes, and how each plant species adapted itself to survive in an environment in which all life forms competed for dominance. He lifted a sinuous brown vine attached to a tuberous root on one end and a withered trumpet shape on the other.

"Take this, for example. The lovely wild potato."

"Potato!" Micky laughed at the sight. "It looks more like a French fry!"

"Don't laugh, young man." Josh spoke in such thunderous tones that the boys all giggled more. "The wild potato is an excellent example of adaptation. It grows in almost any kind of a field, it has a lovely flower that attracts bees and butterflies for pollination, it grows on these long lovely vines to ensure that it can climb up out of the usual muck and get sunshine, and it grows from these strong, tuberous roots."

"Don't animals try to eat the roots?" Micky asked. "We have a mole in our backyard and Dad says it tries to eat plant roots."

"Well, as a matter of fact, animals do try to eat these roots, but they also end up loosening the soil, and letting more tubers grow more easily."

"I don't get it," Robbie complained.

"Think of an ecosystem as a big sports arena," Rebecca suggested.

"You mean like the OSU stadium?" Micky, the inveterate Buckeye fan, asked. "These"—he held up the tuber—"are the Buckeyes, and these"—he pinched a tiny coreopsis seed—"are the Michigan Wolverines!" He laughed gleefully at the thought of the pummeling the heavy potato root would give the tiny coreopsis. "The Buckeyes win again!"

"Well, it's not exactly like that." Rebecca shook her head. "It's more like a big stadium where there are about a hundred teams playing all at once, and some are playing football, while others are playing soccer, baseball, basketball, and hockey. And not only that, but the teams that are playing against each other in football can use the basketball players to carry their ball some of the time."

"Yeah," Josh added, "but the baseball players can also get knocked out by a stray hockey puck sometimes, too."

The sports analogy proved to be too much temptation for the boys, who started throwing seeds at each other and then diving behind a stack of hay bales to avoid return fire. Within seconds, the placid sorting process degenerated into a free-for-all on the barn floor, and Rebecca held her breath waiting for the seeds to go flying. Fortunately, Josh managed, with no apparent effort, to keep the boys' antics contained to an area away from the work. He grabbed each of them for several tosses in the hay, tickled them until they were exhausted from laughter, and finally picked Micky up by the heels and walked him upside down across the barn floor.

"Ha!" The sound exploded beside Rebecca. "Ha!" Patty erupted with another exclamation. Rebecca faced her niece, whose stare focused about a yard above the play between her cousin and Josh. "Micky hand feet! Ha!"

Rebecca could hardly breathe, she felt so stunned. Was Patty actually laughing? Was she laughing with Micky? Had she actually put three . . . three . . . words together to form a concept?

"Micky hand feet!"

By this time, Micky's face had turned the shade of the Red Rome apples in the orchard, and Josh turned him back upright. After a few calming minutes straightening the hay bales, Josh corralled the three boys back to the table where they resumed their sorting. Rebecca remained breathless, not even certain now that she had heard Patty correctly. Patty, meanwhile, returned to play with her piles of seeds.

Josh glanced at Rebecca's frozen face and smiled. He had heard Patty, too, and he wondered if the words were as significant as he thought. He walked casually around the work area, praising the boys and making his way toward Rebecca.

"Keep breathing," he reminded her gently as he placed a reassuring hand on her shoulder. "I wouldn't want to have to hold you up by your ankles to get the blood back to your brain."

"Did you hear?" she asked. Her eyes widened in hope and fear.

"Yes. Does it mean as much as I think it does?"

Rebecca stared at Patty's bent head. "I don't know. But it was two firsts at once."

Josh watched Patty's hands instead of her head. She worked so methodically, so patiently, her moaning noise almost completely transformed into a kind of tuneless humming now. She carefully selected a brown pod of everlasting peas and placed it beside another of the same type. Slowly she found still another pod and moved it to sit with the first two. He realized that she had already made a carefully formed pile of all the two-toned coreopsis seeds in front of her.

"Rebecca." Josh frowned in surprise. "Has Patty done this work before?"

"No. I just thought she would like the feel of the seeds."

"Look." He moved slowly, as if afraid he might upset some precarious balance if he spoke or moved too quickly. "These are sorted by type in groups of twenty."

Rebecca looked at Patty's piles of seeds, which continued to show even more organization, and this time she almost did forget to breathe. These little miracles of organizing behavior occurred more often than verbal communication, but Rebecca still found them extraordinary.

"Patty." She felt like shouting, but she actually spoke quite calmly. "You are doing a very good job. Do you want to put this pile in an envelope now?"

Patty ignored her and kept working, but said, "Two hundred twenty-seven."

"Patty!" The little girl didn't look up from her

seeds. Rebecca scraped the stack of coreopsis into an envelope without eliciting any reaction from Patty and shrugged with a smile. "Good job, Patty!"

"Two hundred twenty-seven."

"She's counting them. That's what she does, but she also sorted them correctly," Rebecca whispered.

Josh remained standing behind Rebecca for a few minutes, his hand still on her shoulder. Cold November sunlight filtered through the slats of the barn, long rays containing no heat but glinting off the floating dust motes until the entire room seemed to glow with a soft, golden shine. He could feel the few quiet tears sliding down Rebecca's cheeks, even though he stood behind her and she made no sound. More than anything in the world, he wanted to wrap her in his arms and share the sweet surge of wonder at Patty's tiny, extraordinary successes.

He placed his other hand on her shoulder, too, and leaned down until his cheek brushed the side of her hair and his mouth pressed gently against her ear. Squeezing her shoulders he whispered, "I know."

Rebecca actually allowed a tiny sob to escape then, but she swallowed the rest of her tears back down. She couldn't stop herself from sinking a little against Josh's strong arms, and when he laid his cheek against the top of her head she let her weight rest back against his chest. Watching the children working happily, feeling Josh's steady heartbeat, she felt more contentment than she had known for a long time. All of her good intentions about remaining detached were forgotten for the moment.

It couldn't last, of course. Danny had to go to the bathroom, and Josh volunteercd to take him back to the house. They brought back cookies and hot chocolate on a tray, and the sorting process continued for nearly another hour, but the sedentary activity couldn't hold the boys any longer. Patty seemed content to continue sorting, so Rebecca remained and worked with her; meanwhile, Josh piled Micky, Robbie, and Danny into his truck and drove them to the hardware store where he bought wire for fence repairs at one of his sites.

By the end of the day, Rebecca could hardly believe how well things had gone. With Josh there to help handle the children, the normal conflicts and problems of the day didn't turn into crises and catastrophes. Even with two adults, caring for these four children required a tremendous amount of energy, but Rebecca marveled at how much easier things were than when she handled them alone. When finally they all sat down to dinner, she realized the day had actually been fun.

Patty had laughed several more times. Once the boys realized what her unusual burst of sound meant, they outdid themselves trying to be funny. Their slapstick attempts at humor didn't work, but Patty surprised them all by making her own joke. The boys were raking the few remaining leaves from the large buckeye tree in the front yard and Patty walked around searching the ground. Then she picked up a smooth, brown-and-tan sphere which she held up for all to see. "Ha! Micky!" she shouted. Everyone looked at her, waiting. "Ha! Micky!" she yelled again, pointing to the nut she held in her hand but staring at the ground in front of her feet.

Suddenly Josh laughed. "Patty, you told a joke!"

"What? What?" The boys jumped in excitement.

"Patty says that's you, Micky. You're a Buckeye!"

Of course the work party dissolved into a wild scramble for more buckeyes at that point, but Rebecca couldn't have cared less. Her Patty had made a joke. She had remembered Micky's words about the Ohio State Buckeyes. She had made a connection between the words, this object, her cousin, and the fact that it was funny. It might not be the Marx Brothers, but it was definitely humor. Rebecca's heart sang.

Now they all sat down to a dinner of fried chicken, mashed potatoes, and peas. When Patty began picking up her peas and counting them according to size, Rebecca let herself laugh along with the others instead of worrying about Colleen's reaction to Patty's persevering behavior. The mood of the evening remained easygoing and Josh insisted that he and the boys would clean the kitchen while Rebecca helped Patty with her bath.

"They've been so good today, I might even try to take them all to church tomorrow," Rebecca said with a smile when she and Josh finally sat down for a cup of coffee while the boys played a final computer game. "It's probably a mistake, but I would like to go."

"If we go together, we can probably manage," Josh suggested. "I think we make a pretty good team."

Rebecca felt a snag of anxiety begin to tug at her, but she forced herself free from it. "I think so, too. And I want to thank you, again. I don't know why you wanted to be here all day, but I'm glad you were."

"Rebecca, you know I've always wanted—"

The loud ring of the telephone interrupted him, and Rebecca rose to answer it. Denise was calling to talk to the boys before she and Mike left for the ballet. Robbie cried a little for his mother after the phone call, but Josh's promise of a bedtime story distracted all the boys enough to get them through teeth brushing, pajamas, and prayers. While Josh read, Rebecca answered another phone call.

"Is she any better?" Colleen's voice sounded hesitant, guilty, and defensive all at once.

"Oh, Colleen, you won't believe what happened!" Rebecca practically shouted into the phone. "She laughed! And she used three words! And she sorted seeds according to type! And she—"

Colleen broke into Rebecca's excitement with an unexpected harshness. "Stop it, Bitsy. I know what you're trying to do and it won't work. Chuck called Cambridge today. The administrator wasn't there, but one of the staff said that Patty sounds like she would fit right in. The director is going to call us back on Monday and we're going to schedule a visit right away. I'm not going to go through any more of this." Colleen's words tumbled out too quickly for Rebecca to slip any argument in. "I just want you to keep her this one last weekend, Bitsy. That's all. Then you won't ever have to take care of her again."

Rebecca felt her stomach tighten in a knot of pain. "Colleen, you need to think this over."

"I already have. I just called to let you know what's going on. If you can just keep her until we get this visit scheduled, then we'll handle everything from there."

"But Colleen . . ."

"Don't worry about it, Bits. Chuck will take care of it."

"Colleen!" Frustration flooded Rebecca as her sister ignored her.

"Give Mom a message for me, and have her call

me when they get in tomorrow, Bits. Thanks.''

The line went dead and Rebecca slammed down the receiver as all semblance of control deserted her. She wanted to break something, and she lifted the heavy cast-iron skillet from the stove and heaved it across the room just as Josh walked into its path.

Although they made it to church the next morning, and the children even managed to sit relatively still for most of the service, Rebecca didn't concentrate as much on the sermon as she did on the ugly bruising on the side of Josh's face. He also had been forced to tape up a couple of fingers damaged when he warded off her missile, but Rebecca counted that as a blessing since those fingers had protected his eye. She couldn't remember ever being so humiliated before, and she couldn't even blame it on anyone else.

When John and Mary Mason joined their son at the end of the pew, Rebecca greeted them with an enthusiastic friendliness designed to camouflage her feelings of guilt. She worried so much about their reaction to Josh's injury that she failed to notice how intently they watched her. By the end of the service, Rebecca wanted only to escape without too much embarrassment.

As they left the steepled brick building, several parishioners stopped Josh to ask him about his injury, but Rebecca kept the children walking toward the parking lot. She didn't know how he would explain it, but she didn't think she could tolerate hearing him speak either the truth or a lie. Eventually he caught up with them and they started back to the farm.

''What did your parents say?'' she finally asked.

''They just wanted to know what happened.''

''What did you tell them?''

"I just told them the truth." He grinned mischievously.

"Oh." In spite of herself she realized she had expected him to be a bit more chivalrous than that.

"I said we were working out at the farm and your sister threw something heavy to you. When you tossed it to me, I wasn't ready to catch it. . . . I also said I should have seen it coming because I had been expecting it all day."

Rebecca caught her breath, torn between crying and laughing. Finally she let the laughter win. "You know what, Dr. Mason? You're wonderful."

"Why, thank you, Ms. Traynor. I'll remember that you said that, the next time I'm trying to catch your frying pan."

Chapter Seven

Rebecca remembered her words every time he did something else wonderful over the next few weeks. She decided to ask Cindy White to have her students sort the remaining seeds in class, and Josh helped her make packets of identification materials. Together they transplanted some good-sized bulrush plants to help hold the soil along the edge of the ponds, and they laid a fine mesh screen over grass seed in the hope that some growth might occur in the few remaining weeks of autumn.

Against his advice, Rebecca spent hours of back-breaking labor carrying open-worked paving stones around one side of the pond and then prayed that grass would come through the holes. Josh complained that the paving stones detracted from the natural roughness of the area, but he really worried that the work demanded too much physical strength. Rebecca simply flexed her muscles and laughed at him. She knew that the wheelchair bound students would be able to navigate on the paving stones, but not on the mesh-covered earth, and she wanted these children to have access to as much of the area as possible.

Rebecca still traveled to the city for her work at the nursing home once a week, but with the advent of really cold weather she spent most of her time on the construction of the boardwalks. Josh managed to help her at least part of every day, even though he had his hands full with his own administrative duties and research.

With the last of the autumn leaves gone, there were days when the only color she saw was gray: gray sky, gray water, gray mud, gray boards being held together by gray nails. She wouldn't have minded so much, if she didn't also have a gray cloud hanging over her head in the form of Colleen's plan to place Patty in the institution. Colleen and Chuck's visit to the home in Cambridge had been delayed because of Chuck's schedule, but Rebecca knew that Colleen had not given up the idea. Rebecca worried the thought like a dog with an unwieldy bone, as she gripped a nail in her icy fingers and hammered the last pieces in the railing at one end of the boardwalk.

For now, Patty remained with Rebecca on the farm, attending her special school most days, and working with Rebecca some of the time. The little girl had gone with Rebecca to the high school to help with the seed sorting activity, and she had astonished the students with her ability to accurately count three and four piles of seeds at the same time. Patty's ability to count and organize patterns far exceeded the average six-year-old's. Why couldn't Colleen appreciate it?

"Isn't it getting a little cold for you to be doing this?" Josh's voice carried out to her from the parking lot. "Why don't you call it a day?"

"Hi!" She gave the last nail a few more whacks and put her tools back into her case. "I'm finished for now, but I have to come back tomorrow and start on the other side."

Josh joined her at the end of the walkway and gazed at the ponds. "Sure doesn't look like much yet, does it?"

"Gray," she said succinctly.

"Yeah. But I have an idea of what might help it in the spring."

"What?" She felt her spirits lift immediately. His ideas were always good.

"Your plan calls for heavy foliage around the edge of the ponds, but with all that we had to cut down for the dredging, your tree line is pretty far away from the water now."

"I know. That's why I got the bulrushes and the sedges."

He nodded. "But I think you need something taller and fuller up close to the water's edge."

She felt a little prick of territoriality. After all, the plant scheme was supposed to be hers. "I like the idea of open space near the water's edge, because the students will be able to get all the way down to check out the water plants."

"I agree. But not necessarily all the way around the pond. We can have some excellent nesting sites for some of our rare species of warblers if we plant this right, and willows would grow very quickly. Don't you think your students would enjoy bird-watching while they're gardening?"

Thinking about it, she decided he was right. "On the far side of the ponds, though, not here where the trees would block the view from the walkway."

"Yes. What do you think?"

She nodded with enthusiasm. "We could plant them very soon, too. Willows need to go in during the winter."

"I just happen to have a mature growth of willow trees at the Grove Marsh site; we could take some cuttings there in early January if the weather's cold enough."

She smiled. "We do make a good team."

"We always did."

As always, any mention of the past left her looking a little wary, but Josh took some comfort in the fact that this time she didn't suddenly distance herself with that overly polite voice of hers. Instead, she leaned against her newly built railing and told him about her worries.

"Colleen says they've finally scheduled their visit to Cambridge. She still won't listen to me talk about Patty's accomplishments. She didn't even care that I was able to take Patty with me to my class the other day. Patty didn't just count seeds this time; she helped plant seeds for the indoor experiments on light and water, and she actually handed out seeds to the students who aren't ambulatory. Colleen didn't care at all."

"She's afraid to listen to you. She's afraid she'll change her mind, or start to hope again."

"I know. It's so sad, though. She *should* have hope about these things. These are realistic. She could appreciate Patty for who she is, not complain about who she isn't."

Josh stood behind her at the rail, remembering the morning in the barn. That day, everything had been golden. Today, everything was gray. But when he listened to Rebecca, when he heard her soft, thoughtful voice strung tight with sadness, he wanted to pull her against him again so he could give her at least the comfort of his arms. He stepped up beside her and put a brotherly arm around her shoulder the way he had done when she was a young girl. "You are a good sister, Ms. Rebecca Traynor," he said.

"Thanks." She sighed as she leaned a sisterly head against his chest. "You know, I have to admit, I like the fact that at least you always remember who I am."

Three weeks later Rebecca found herself once again finishing a section of the boardwalk, this time the final section. The skies were still gray and the air was cold, but Rebecca hummed as she worked. Thanksgiving had come and gone, and Rebecca gave special thanks that Patty remained at the farm and continued to do well. The little girl spent most of her time either in school or with her aunt, but today she had stayed with her grandparents.

Rebecca stretched and searched the sky for some hint of the sun. She thought it was about mid-afternoon, but she had left her watch at home and she could only say that she was fairly certain the sun had not yet set because she could still see her hammer. With so little sunlight this fall none of the grass she and Josh had planted had come up, and Rebecca anticipated that they would need to reseed in the spring. Oh, well, it would be a good experience for the students.

A movement caught her attention and she watched

Josh saunter through the field to the opposite end of the boardwalk. Some days now he managed to look at her construction without cringing, and he hadn't actually complained a single time since she agreed to plant the willows. As he stepped onto the planks, a slight shift in the cloud cover allowed a brightening of the sky, and Rebecca heard herself saying, "You brighten up my day." Immediately she prayed that he hadn't heard her.

"Why, thank you, Ms. Traynor," he responded with comic gallantry. "I must say, you do a lot for mine, too."

She laughed at the flirtation but stuck some nails in her mouth and bent to her task so she wouldn't have to keep it up. Things were going great between them as long as she didn't let herself start feeling too much.

"Things are looking pretty good, Rebecca. In spite of the fact that nothing's growing this time of the year. You've done a good job."

"Mammss," she thanked him with her mouth full of nails.

"You talk real good, too . . . for a farm girl." He tossed out the old, familiar insult with ease.

Rebecca considered testing the strength of his boots with her hammer, but decided she didn't want him to explain another set of bruises at church. Instead she just kept pounding nails for a few minutes. Then she cocked her head and leaned a little closer toward the edge of the boardwalk. She held the pose, then leaned farther, gasped a little, and held completely still.

"What?" Josh whispered. "What is it?"

Rebecca shook her head and removed the remaining nails from her mouth. "Shh!" She leaned farther and felt Josh leaning, too. He strained forward, peering intently over the edge of the boardwalk until he was overbalanced just enough for Rebecca's purposes. With an easy shove she sent him over the edge into the half-dried mud of the pond bank.

"Made you look . . . city slicker!" She burst out laughing at her ability to catch him in that ludicrous prank they used to play on each other. Her laughter was cut short as he grabbed her foot and pulled her down on top of him. "Hey!"

"All's fair once you knock me into the mud, farm girl!"

"Okay! Okay! We're even now." She laughed, holding her hands up in appeasement. "But I can't believe you let me sucker you into that, Mason. You used to be much smarter."

He let himself have a brief fantasy of throwing her into the mud and wrestling the sass out of her, but the image got dangerous as soon as he thought of her wrapped in his arms and rolling around, so he let it go. "You're in a fine mood today. Are you glad to be finished with this?"

"Nearly finished," she corrected him. "I still have more work to do. But I am in a good mood."

"Any particular reason?"

Rebecca thought about the easy passage of Thanksgiving and nodded. "I'm just feeling more hopeful that Colleen may change her mind. The holiday went great for Patty, and Mom and Dad had a big, long, hush-hush talk with Colleen and Chuck. I think maybe they've convinced her that it's okay for them to leave Patty out at the farm all the time."

Josh frowned a little. "Do you really think your parents can give Patty what she needs?"

Rebecca shrugged her shoulders and returned to her

nails. "No. But I think *I* can. I take care of Patty most of the time now, anyway, and if I just plan for it, I can care for her full-time."

"You can't plan for emergencies."

"Of course not." She pulled a small cell phone out of her jacket pocket and Josh hoped he hadn't damaged it when he pulled her onto the ground. "I'll just be like all the other working-mom types. I'll take care of emergencies when they arise."

Josh snatched the phone from her hand and admired it. "Does this go on your expense account?"

Her playful mood returned along with his and she stuck out her tongue at him. "As far as I can tell, the only kind of expense account I have is the one where the hardware salesman gives me an account of how expensive everything is."

"That sounds about right." He turned on the phone and listened to the dial tone. "It works."

"Of course it works. Who sounds like a farm kid now?"

Josh thought about how much it cost to have a phone like this and how little money Rebecca actually made. "You really do love that kid, don't you?" he mused, his mood suddenly serious again. "Not everybody could."

Unwilling to let him see the intensity of her response, Rebecca pounded in another nail. After a few minutes of silence she gave him the only answer she could. "I love plants, too. They don't love me back, they don't talk to me, they don't even really grow for me. I can tend them and sometimes help them grow better, but the relationship is really pretty one-sided. It's not completely one-sided with Patty, but it's not your run-of-the-mill mutual admiration club."

She shrugged her shoulders again, that gesture that seemed to have become so much a part of her, indicating a kind of obstinate fatalism. "Maybe that's the only kind of relationship I'm good at: the one-sided kind."

Then, because it was too close to how she had always felt about him, she pounded the next nail too hard and bent it before it was halfway into the board. With a cry, she tried to pry it out and smashed her index finger in the process.

"Let me help," Josh said in that quiet way he had. He set the phone down away from the edge of the boardwalk, took the hammer from her, and straightened the nail before he levered it out of the wood.

He handed back the hammer and put the nail in his pocket. "I want to tell you something." They were both sitting on the edge of the boardwalk where it wound close to the water and it felt like being on a pier at the lake, except that there was hardly any water and hardly any pier.

"This place is ugly as sin." He sighed. "I think about my messy jungle that was here before and I could cry because this place is so torn up now, but I don't feel that way for long. Do you know why?"

She shook her head silently, gazing at the pitiful pond.

"Because I know that you will take care of it. You are the most careful person I have ever known in my life, Rebecca Traynor. Careful . . . full of care. When you were eleven years old you took care of your whole family, and you're still doing it." He touched her cheek and turned her face toward him. "You took care of every bird, cat, and puppy you could find. You even took care of me."

Rebecca's eyes narrowed as she searched for the mockery in his words. "What do you mean?" She ignored the warmth where his hand lingered on her cheek.

"I know your sisters teased you about hanging around me all the time, but they didn't understand anything. You and I both know that I was the one always hanging around you."

"Oh yeah, right." She used the words as a shield, protecting herself from the unnamed fear that began to curl around her heart.

"Rebecca, I mean it." Grabbing her hand, he squeezed it for emphasis. "I have always thought of you as my friend. Right from the beginning. Even when you *were* just a little kid, I didn't think of you as just a little kid. I thought of you as this really interesting person who had a lot to share with me." He swallowed and pushed himself on, continuing to cup her cheek so that she stared directly into his eyes. "And the older you got, the more interesting you were." He watched the rose flush rising up her neck and knew it probably mirrored his own, but he was in this for good now and he wasn't going to let old habits stop him.

"In fact, Rebecca," he whispered as he leaned close enough to touch her with his mouth. He brushed his lips softly over the hair at her temple. "Now, you're—"

The metallic chirping of the cell phone momentarily interrupted his thought.

"Now, you're—"

The ringing persisted. Josh grumbled and reached for the phone. "What is it with telephones? I think

I'm cursed. I suppose you'd better answer it, since you got it for emergencies."

Rebecca couldn't speak. Her throat had closed like the hole of a sand lizard in the Sahara Desert: dry, tight, and safe. She waved a fluttery hand at Josh to indicate that he should take the call.

It was Faye, and she sounded upset when she heard him answer. "Josh?" Her familiar voice broke through. "Joshua Mason?"

Josh coughed and hoped his own voice had returned to normal. "Yes, Faye. It's Josh."

"This is Faye. Faye Traynor." She repeated her name as if he could possibly not know who she was. "I . . . oh dear, I hate these things . . . I must have called the wrong number. Well, I need to speak with Bitsy . . . I know she's out at the pond—at least I think that's where she is—but I have an emergen . . . well, it's not really an emergency, but I do need to find Bitsy and I thought, well, if you go out to the pond you could tell her. But you probably won't go unless you're already there . . . oh, dear . . . well, I'm sorry. . . ."

Josh broke into the confused verbiage. "It's all right, Faye. I'm here with Rebecca. Just tell me what's wrong."

"Well . . ." Rebecca's mother gasped a little sob. "I just need to find Bitsy. Colleen and Chuck are coming to pick up Patty, and I think Bitsy should be here."

Rebecca sat silently watching him, not able to hear her mother, but knowing from Josh's expression that the crisis was probably real and not imagined.

"Don't worry, Faye. I'll make sure that Rebecca gets home right away."

"Oh, thank you, Josh. You have always been such

a wonderful boy. I could always count on you to take care of Bitsy.''

''Uh . . . yeah. Thanks.'' Josh suppressed the instinctive flash of guilt he felt and rushed through his next words. ''We'll be there as soon as we can.''

He would have given everything he had ever owned, everything he had ever done, and everything he had ever been to be able to protect her from this. ''I'm sorry. It's Patty. They're taking her.''

They stared at each other across the space that separated them, and Rebecca found the name of her fear. Josh watched her withdraw into that place of isolation, and he thought that if she used her polite voice on him now he might be driven crazy. He didn't give her the chance; he just pulled her to her feet and then followed her home in his truck.

Chapter Eight

"Don't start with me, Bitsy!" Colleen shouted at her sister as she threw Patty's sweatpants and sweatshirts into a large suitcase. "It's all settled, and you aren't going to make me feel guilty about it." Patty sat in the middle of her trundle bed, rocking back and forth and moaning softly to herself. "Just look at her! She needs to be someplace where she can be helped."

Rebecca took another deep breath, something she had been doing before each effort she made to speak with her sister. "Colleen, I just think you should take your time with this. Give all of us a chance to adjust to it."

Colleen slammed the suitcase shut and whirled around to face Rebecca. "No! You just stay out of it You don't have to think about anyone but yourself, Bitsy. You think you can give me advice about what to do, but I know what I have to do. I have to think about Chuck and Shelly. I have to think about other people. I'm not like you. I'm not single and carefree. I have responsibilities. I just can't take care of Patty and everyone else, too.''

The injustice of Colleen's accusation didn't even penetrate, since the only thing Rebecca could think about was losing her niece.

''Colleen, let the family help you and Chuck.''

''No.'' Colleen picked up the suitcase and started out the door. ''Come on, Patty!''

''But why?'' Rebecca pleaded.

Colleen put down the suitcase again, returned to the bed, and grabbed Patty's hand to pull her out the door. Patty moaned a little louder, but she didn't resist her mother's pull.

''Colleen, why?''

''She isn't getting any better with you.'' Without letting Rebecca reply, Colleen wrestled the suitcase and her daughter down the stairs and out the front door where Chuck waited for her. His face held the same sad determination as Colleen's, and he took the suit-case without a word. Bob and Faye stood near the car, but Lindsey and Caitlin didn't even leave the house. They stood at the window watching the scene in silence.

''Colleen!'' Rebecca rushed past her sister and planted herself in front of them. ''At least let me say good-bye to her.''

Colleen halted then and released Patty's hand with a wave as if to say ''go ahead.'' With one final deep breath, Rebecca tried to calm herself before she knelt in front of her niece.

''Patty? Patty, I am going to give you a hug. I know you don't like it much, but it will just be a little hug.''

Patty kept her eyes on the ground and held herself stiffly while Rebecca quickly squeezed her thin shoulders. She did not pull away, scream, or flail her arms, and Rebecca closed her eyes with the thought that all this extraordinary progress would evaporate if Patty left.

"Good-bye, Patty," she whispered.

"There. You see? She can't even hug you back. She can't even do that! Don't you see why we have to take her away?" Colleen's control was disappearing rapidly, and she shoved Patty into the backseat of the car.

Rebecca felt something go dead in her heart. In all the years of being overlooked as the little lost girl in the middle of the Traynor clan, she had never felt such pain as this. Never had her own feelings been so devastatingly overlooked. She went to the place in her heart where no one could hurt her. She wouldn't be angry—that never helped; she wouldn't cry—no one would notice. The silence held her.

Now that Rebecca had stopped arguing, Colleen relaxed enough to be somewhat more gracious. "Thank you for taking care of her these past weeks while we finalized the arrangements, Mom. I know she's been a handful."

Faye waved to her granddaughter with a little smile on her face. "Oh, she's never any trouble to me, Colleen. We're going to miss her. She and Bitsy get along just fine." She spoke as if the two were playmates, and Colleen nodded in agreement.

"Well, Bitsy can go to the home to visit Patty any time she wants. This is the address." She handed her mother a card, which Faye passed on to Rebecca. "Good-bye, Bitsy." Colleen said good-bye to her father and then realized that Josh stood at the porch railing watching the scene. "Oh, Josh. I didn't know you were there. I'm sorry you had to see all this, but don't worry. The home is a good place for Patty. Bitsy will understand someday."

He couldn't even respond to Colleen's ridiculous assumption that Rebecca didn't understand. All he could see was the cold distance on Rebecca's face. As the car pulled out of the yard, he crossed to Rebecca's side and put a comforting arm around her; she remained as stiff and disconnected as Patty.

"Rebecca."

The face she turned toward his was devoid of any expression other than a mild interest. "Yes?"

"Are you going to be all right?"

"Of course. I'll finish up the last of the railing tomorrow. Once I start my indoor work with the school, I won't have as much time to get out to the site."

"It's that voice." He thought he might actually hate Colleen for bringing this sound to him again.

"Yes. I guess it is. So sorry." She didn't sound sorry at all.

"Rebecca."

"Do you have my tools?"

"Don't do this. Please. We'll do something for her. We'll visit her. We'll get Colleen to change her mind."

"No. I don't think we will. It's a shame, but what can you do?" She turned away from him and started toward the house. "Just leave the tools on the porch. I'll get them later."

"Rebecca!" This day couldn't end like this. Not after what they had had. He had been so close to finally telling her how he felt. But she walked through the front door as if she hadn't heard him.

Bob and Faye, arms entwined, watched the scene without comment until Josh stomped off to retrieve her belt of tools and her nails, then Bob turned to Faye and whispered something in her ear. She nodded thoughtfully and called for Caitlin.

Just as Josh set the belt on the porch Caitlin bounded out the front door and ran into him.

"Oops! Sorry, Josh. What is it, Mom?"

"Well, dear, I wondered if you might want to ask Josh to help you with your driving. I know your father said he'd help you this evening, but it's already time for him to do the milking, and since Josh is here, maybe he could help."

Josh stared at Faye for a minute in anger and confusion until she continued. "And if he helped you for a little while, then he could stay for supper. I'll go get started on it right now." When she looked back at him, her face twitched in something suspiciously close to a wink.

"Would you, Josh?" Caitlin begged. "I'm supposed to get my learner's permit in two weeks and I don't even know how to use a gearshift yet. Just let me drive around the barnyard a few times."

. Josh kept his eyes on Rebecca's parents. "If you're sure you want me to, Faye," Josh answered slowly. "I might not be as patient as you think."

Bob laughed and squeezed his wife. "Boy, you've been coming around this henhouse for more years than I can remember, without ever losing your temper with one of my girls, and that means you're more patient than any one man has a right to be. You just teach Caitlin how to drive, and we'll feed you supper for a month. Supper . . . right here . . . in the house . . . for a month."

Josh's confusion resolved into something different, something more like certainty. They knew. They knew that he loved Rebecca. They'd probably known for years and just hadn't interfered before today. Now they were taking a stand, and it wasn't to keep him away. They approved of him. He thought of his father's face filled with worry and determination, and he thought of how long ago all that had been. He smiled. "A month? That sounds just about right. I ought to be able to teach a girl a lot in a month."

"No matter how stubborn she is," Bob agreed.

"Hey! I'm not stubborn!" Caitlin complained.

"Of course not," Josh mollified her. "Now get in the truck and show me what you know."

Supper consisted of ten parts food, five parts teasing Caitlin about stripping the gears on Josh's truck, and one part (Rebecca's part) painfully correct manners. No one spoke of Patty. With an effort, Josh reminded himself that he was supposed to be patient, then ignored Rebecca's protests and helped her wash the dishes. When the last pans were safely stowed in their proper places, he pulled the towel out of her hands and trapped her around the waist with it.

"Are you upset about what I was saying to you this afternoon?" he asked without a preamble. He didn't touch her at all, but restrained her with the towel and didn't let her back away.

Rebecca closed her eyes, distancing herself with her shuttered lids.

"Rebecca, I need to know this. I know this isn't at the top of your list of problems right now, but if I hurt you or offended you somehow, I need to know it. I can't just pretend it didn't happen."

She breathed heavily, sucking in her feelings along with the air, biting her lips to hold in whatever words wanted to escape. Finally she trusted herself to open her eyes and look at him.

"Nothing happened."

"Okay," he agreed with a frown. "I'll buy that, if you say so. So why did you decide to go live on another planet all of a sudden?"

She closed her eyes, shutting him out again. "It was a mistake."

"A mistake? What was a mistake?" He heard his voice rising and fought it back down. "Why was it a mistake?"

"Can't you guess? Can't you understand? It's just like with Patty. That was a mistake, too."

Josh reeled her in a little closer with the dish towel. "No. I don't understand." He put his hand under her chin and searched her face, but she held her eyes tightly shut. "I don't understand why you would take all that hurt and anger and then hold it to yourself like some kind of treasure that you are hoarding. I don't understand why you wouldn't let me share it with you."

A look of anger flashed across her face and she opened her eyes in defiance. "That's just how Colleen feels about Patty. She expects Patty to share all of her feelings. When she can't do it, Colleen gets hurt and angry and blames Patty." Rebecca pulled away with enough force to tear the towel out of Josh's hands, and it fluttered to the floor. "But it's not Patty's fault. It's the autism. It's one of the symptoms. 'A lack of spontaneous sharing . . . a lack of emotional reciprocity.'" She quoted the words as if they were a curse. "It doesn't make any sense to be angry with her, because that's the way she's made!''

Calmly Josh lifted the dish towel from the floor and folded it over the edge of the counter. He waited for her to continue, but Rebecca simply backed up another step and crossed her arms in a defensive stance. He shoved his own hands into his pockets rather than reach out. He wasn't certain if he would embrace her or shake her in frustration.

"Are you saying that's the way you're made, Rebecca? Are you trying to tell me that you're not able to share feelings and relationships any more than Patty is?" He kept his tone soft, trying to work past his own hurt to hers. "Because if you are, I don't believe you. I know you can come out from behind that wall of yours. Patty may shut out the rest of the world because that's the way her brain is wired, but you do it because it's your choice."

She shook her head. "I do it because every time I ever let someone get close, I get hurt. I'm not supposed to have someone special to love."

"Rebecca." Josh felt sick from the tightness in his gut. He wasn't even sure what he should be arguing for, but he knew one thing about her feelings with absolute certainty. One thing that had nothing to do with him. "You know you love Patty."

"Of course I love Patty. I loved her from the minute she was born. When Colleen couldn't stand to hold her because she was so stiff and inconsolable, I loved her. I didn't care if she couldn't cuddle like other babies, I just loved her."

Insistent tears started to seep out past the barriers, but Rebecca ignored them. "I loved her when she didn't like being sung to, when she hated being rocked, and when she would watch her own fingers for an hour as if she held the secrets of the universe there. I loved her when she learned to count, and she counted everything, all day long over and over. Colleen would start to cry, but I just wanted to listen to Patty count. She was like this wonderful, interesting creature. Not like anybody else in the entire world. She just kept unfolding like an amazing flower. She couldn't hug, or hold on, or tell you about what she experienced, but she just kept growing in her own way."

Rebecca stood in the middle of the kitchen, hugging herself and gently rocking in a rhythm reminiscent of Patty's stereotyped movements, tears streaming down her face now, but not making any move toward the anguished man before her.

"I loved her when she counted those peas, and I loved her when she told that joke. . . ." Rebecca choked, sobbed, and her head fell forward onto her chest. "Oh, Josh, she told a joke. She *told a joke*. How much more social interaction can you want? How could they take her away?"

She couldn't talk anymore then, and Josh moved to encircle her with his arms. He held her tightly and whispered over and over how he knew and he was sorry and he understood. He didn't try to tell her that everything would be all right, because he knew it wouldn't; but his own heart lightened with the joy of being allowed back inside her walls even a little. For the first time, he sympathized with the pain Colleen must feel, believing that she would never make it inside Patty's walls.

They stayed there in the kitchen for a long time, with Josh just holding her, and Rebecca not resisting;

but after a while, she wrapped her arms around him and held him back. Through the pain, she recognized a flicker of gratitude that no one called to her to make the coffee.

When Josh let himself out of the house much later, Bob and Faye didn't even look up from the television show they were watching from the living room sofa, but Faye sighed heavily and leaned her head on her husband's shoulder.

"Now don't you worry, Faye. Everything's going to work out just fine."

"It better." She nudged him sharply. "I still feel guilty about leaving her here that weekend with all those children."

"I told you he'd show up to help her out, didn't I? Just like I knew he'd take her off alone that first night he came back, if I insulted her enough. Just like I knew he'd stick around for supper tonight, if we gave him an excuse. I've got everything under control."

"That's what you said when you introduced her to that Johnson boy from Plain City. He took her on those wild motorcycle rides for two months and never came back after she smacked him for getting fresh."

Bob chuckled unrepentantly. "Isn't that the truth? I did have everything under control. She got to have some wild memories without ever being in real danger. I always knew she was waiting for Josh to come back, but I figured she should be a teenager while she was waiting. She's always been too much of a mother hen . . . just like you."

"Hmph!"

Chapter Nine

Mixing the perlite, peat moss, and sterilized garden soil in a large can recycled from the food service, Rebecca watched her nursing home clients spreading out the newspapers on their worktables. The residents were starting vegetables from seed and using grow-lamps, with the hope that they could ignore the normal Columbus growing season. Rebecca had suggested that growing foodstuffs might help some of the patients whose appetites were poor. Some of the research suggested that if they felt some personal connection to their veggies, residents would be more enthusiastic about eating. Personal relationships with vegetables sounded good to Rebecca today.

She ladled the potting soil into the various conglomerations of pots, cans, plastic bags, and egg cartons which were collected on the tables and then encouraged each person to select a variety of vegetable seeds based on the pictures covering the packages. Discussion began spontaneously, as most of the residents recognized the foods.

Frank Stoner rubbed his finger back and forth over the luscious photograph of a Big Boy tomato, and his daughter leaned her head against his shoulder.

"I remember that, Dad. You grew those every summer in our backyard, and I would try to find the biggest one. I would wash it off with the hose and eat it like an apple, with the juice dribbling down my shirt. You couldn't keep me out of that tomato patch."

Frank didn't answer, of course. He had lost nearly all semblance of speech over the past few months, but Mary Ann Stoner no longer fought to bring back the father she had known. Instead she watched him relax his stiff muscles and put his hands into a small bucket of soil. She put one of her own fingers in the bucket, too, and Frank rubbed it with dirt.

Rebecca smiled in satisfaction at this evidence of one of the benefits of horticultural therapy. She didn't need to read the results of the Menninger Clinic's research to know that gardening resulted in a reduction of tension and anxiety. The beauty of working with such a nonthreatening medium appealed to her on a personal level as much as a professional one. Yes, relationships with vegetables were about all she could handle today.

She had thrown herself into her work with a vengeance this morning, rushing out to the hard labor of finishing the railing on the boardwalk. After a dash to the hardware store, she had her van filled with various lengths and shapes of PVC pipe for adapting gardening tools for her students. She planned another long evening of labor tonight with the tools, but for now, she reaped the same rewards as these patients when she chose a few tiny radish seeds and gently settled them in her seedling pot. She added some carrot seeds, knowing that the radishes would be out of the way before the carrots grew enough to be crowded.

By the time she sent her charges off for dinner and finished cleaning up the work area, Rebecca had regained some of her lost equilibrium. She watched Mary Ann Stoner kiss her father good-bye and thought wistfully of Patty and Colleen. If only Colleen could learn the kind of acceptance Mary Ann had found. Maybe it was more difficult with a young child whose life lay ahead of her, or maybe it was more difficult to accept the diminishment of a person you had depended on. Maybe comparisons didn't mean a thing. Rebecca shook herself and carried her equipment to her truck.

Christmas shoppers added to the normally hectic traffic, but for once Rebecca waited patiently as the line of cars inched through miles of perpetual construction and chaos. After she had stopped to allow the fourth driver to jump in front of her on the narrowing road, she realized she didn't even want to get home. She dreaded the thought of the long evening ahead, absent her usual hours of working with Patty.

In spite of her reluctance, she eventually made it home and found Caitlin bumping over the frozen ground in Josh's pickup truck. Rebecca parked her van by the barn and began unloading the pipe and hose clamps. By the time she finished and left the barn, the driving lesson had come to a laughing halt.

"Just remember to push the clutch in *before* you try to shift," Josh said, giving Caitlin a little shove into the house and turning to meet Rebecca.

"Hi." He spoke the word with a world of meaning, and blocked her path to the door. "Are you doing okay?"

Rebecca felt herself losing the momentum that had kept her going all day, and panic almost nauseated her. "I . . . sure . . . I . . ." she stammered. "I didn't expect to see you here."

"I didn't think you were paying attention last night when your dad announced that I would be teaching Caitlin how to drive in exchange for a month of suppers."

"A month of . . . ? What?" She really didn't think she could stand any more of his kindness right now. "Well . . ." She didn't know what to say.

"Well. So, hi." He gently grabbed the tips of the fingers on both of her hands and coaxed her toward him. When she stood close, he leaned forward and brushed his lips lightly over hers. "That's all. Just hi." He had never kissed her on the lips before and he wondered if she even noticed. His heart was pounding with the effort to remain nonchalant.

Rebecca rocked back and forth slightly, swaying with her ambivalence, until Josh let go of her fingers and laid his hands on her waist.

"Do you remember learning to drive?" he asked to distract them both.

"I thought I would kill you if you told me one more time to slow down earlier for the stop sign."

"You wouldn't have had the chance. I was going to kill you first!" He felt some small measure of tension drain out of her and he would have drawn her closer, but the door opened and Bob stuck his head out and shouted at them.

"Come on and eat, you two. You can lollygag sometime when the rest of us aren't so hungry!"

Rebecca expected some comment from her father about Josh having his hands on her, but in fact, Bob seemed completely unaware of anything having changed between Josh and Rebecca. After dinner, her mother insisted that she would wash the dishes if Rebecca needed to work. Bob pulled Josh into the living room to discuss Caitlin's driving lessons or "this business of what you're teaching my daughter." Rebecca managed a laugh at Josh's worried expression and escaped to the barn. Josh joined her there a short time later.

"I need to lengthen the tool handles to increase leverage and grip ability for the students. Most of them won't be able to dig effectively if the tools aren't modified," Rebecca explained when she showed Josh her pipe. She pulled out a chart explaining the adaptations needed by each student, and for an hour they used the hose clamps to add straight PVC pipe for length and T-angle PVC pipe for grip options. By the time they were finished, they had an assortment of oddly shaped, but highly effective, tools.

The cool barn seemed even colder as their exertions diminished, and Rebecca shivered when she set her last rake on the pile and stood looking at their work. Josh tossed down a T-handled trowel and smiled from his seat on a bale of hay.

"Want them back in your van?" he asked.

"Not yet. I won't go to the school until day after tomorrow. We're going to use them in the high school greenhouse."

"Those are pretty ingenious tools. I think the kids will be excited."

Rebecca smiled, too—the first genuinely happy

look she'd worn all evening. "I think so. I can't take credit for them, though. I learned about them in a class I took last winter."

"But you applied them to your own situation. You adapted, just like the kids must do."

"Yeah."

"It's a good metaphor. Isn't that what horticultural therapy is supposed to be about? The metaphor of horticulture for life?" Josh watched her closely as he spoke.

"Are you saying that I should find the right metaphor from making these tools?"

He didn't answer.

Rebecca laughed without humor. "Ah. You're saying I should get a grip!"

This time he shook his head. "No. That's what you say to yourself. I say you should use whatever help is offered. You should be willing to adapt to your circumstances." He leaned over and picked up the trowel he had just thrown down. Its new T-shaped handle fit his two-handed grip. "You should be willing to come at things from more than one angle."

"Don't use my own therapy on me, Josh." she grumbled irritably.

"Why not? Don't you believe in it?"

"Of course I do."

He lay the trowel down again and stood up. "Okay. No therapy. Let's lollygag a little." He stretched out a hand and touched her hair. "Everybody's been well fed, so even your dad won't mind."

"He doesn't mind because he knows it's too cold to stay out here for very long."

His arms wrapped around her and drew her close. "Just stay for a little while, then. I'll keep you warm."

Rebecca melted against him as he held her even tighter. The warmth of his breath against her hair spread like a summer breeze until she felt wrapped in the soft cocoon of his caress. The feelings she had kept hidden all day drifted like bubbles to the surface of her heart, bursting when they hit the cold air of awareness, and she suddenly found herself crying with the same deep agony she had had the night before.

Josh held her again, kissing her head and gently rubbing her back, but not moving beyond the bounds of compassion and comfort. The irony didn't escape him that now that he had finally accepted that she was old enough for him, her grief made her much too vulnerable for him to pursue her heart. He kissed the top of her head once more and ignored the fatalism threatening to depress him. It didn't matter. He had been patient for a long time, and he could be patient now.

Rebecca felt herself enfolded by the old comfort, the old familiar Josh who could ease her hurts and show her how to succeed. The friendliness soothed her, but she felt a stabbing pain at the thought of the loss of the romantic involvement they had seemed so near. She had thought she wanted that kind of relationship with him, but now all she wanted was this safe, calm comfort. Maybe they couldn't cross that barrier after all.

With a little hiccup of a sob, Rebecca pulled back slightly and looked at her friend with anguish. ''Josh, what am I going to do?''

He pulled her back against him again for a quick hug and then released her. ''You're going to use all your tools, and you're going to approach things from a different angle.''

* * *

Over the next few weeks, Rebecca tried to discover
the different angle that would help her. She called the
home in Cambridge to ask about Patty's adjustment,
but they wouldn't give her any information over the
phone. She was so angry that she drove all the way to
the school before checking with Colleen, and when
she arrived she was told that the school would not
allow any visitors without the parents' permission.
Colleen and Chuck couldn't be reached and finally Rebecca had to return to Delaware without ever seeing
her niece. At that point, her fury with Colleen grew
until Rebecca felt that she had lost not only her niece,
but her sister as well. Both were so far beyond her
that they might as well have been dead.

"Come on, Rebecca. Just keep digging," Josh encouraged her each evening after dinner. "You'll find
another angle." The T-handled trowel that he had
made went to the high school along with all the other
adapted tools, but one evening he gave her another
that he had made just for her. "Keep it in your van,
just as a reminder," he suggested.

Rebecca drank his encouragement the way a
parched garden soaks up water, but the water had a
bitter tint. If she cried, he comforted her; if she raged,
he calmed her; but he refrained from kissing her again,
and she sometimes thought perhaps she had only
dreamed the afternoon on the boardwalk. Once again
he relegated her to the status of his little friend: his
childish, little friend with whom he had always been
so patient and careful. Part of Rebecca resented this,
but part of her appreciated the fact that she couldn't
possibly respond to anything except her grief.

One Saturday, a few days after her return from the
unsuccessful trip to Cambridge, Rebecca spent the

morning working on Christmas presents for her family. She traditionally potted something for each of them, but this year she had let the time get away from her and she had only a few days left. She had started the calceolarias in June so they would bloom at Christmas, but she had brought them into her cool greenhouse in the barn without potting them separately. Now they were ready to bloom, but they were crowded into one large flat and separating them might endanger their unique, pouchlike blossoms.

She worked steadily, mixing her potting soil carefully and choosing five-inch pots that she had individually decorated for her eight sisters. When she heard the familiar sound of Josh's truck pull into the barnyard, she ignored it and kept working. She assumed he would probably spend some time prepping Caitlin for her written driving exam on Monday before he came looking for Rebecca in the barn; therefore the footsteps behind her startled her when she heard them.

Colleen stood just inside the entrance to the shadowy barn, backlit by the gray December sky behind her. When Rebecca saw her sister, she felt an adrenaline surge that sent her heart into an almost painful thudding and caused her hands to shake. She couldn't identify the emotion that threatened to overwhelm her; she only knew that it was powerful and unpleasant.

"Mom said you were out here." Colleen spoke defiantly. "She said you'd be in the dirt as usual."

Unsure of what to say, Rebecca sunk her fingers into the soil of the flat and began the gentle process of separating a calceolaria from its home.

"And Josh said you might need this . . . whatever it is."

At that, Rebecca raised her head and saw Colleen

holding out the T-handled trowel. Rebecca laid it aside. "It's a trowel, Colleen. I'm sure you've seen one before. When did you see Josh?"

Colleen moved farther into the barn and settled herself on the bale of hay where Josh had sat the night they adapted the tools. "He brought me out."

The calceolaria released its last tentative hold on the soil and relaxed in Rebecca's hand as she lifted it toward the sky-blue pot intended for Caitlin. Keeping her hands gentle and steady, Rebecca digested Colleen's words. "He brought you from your house?"

Colleen frowned and stared out the door. "He called this morning and said he wanted to talk to me. After we talked he brought me out here. I think he's still in the house doing something for Caitlin."

Rebecca molded the potting soil around the calceolaria roots, searching the imminent blooms carefully for any sign of fungus disease. In her present mood, she felt quite certain that the black stains should be evident somewhere, but the blossoms and leaves appeared surprisingly healthy. She watered the plant and set it on a shelf to drain.

"Why did Josh want to talk to you?" Rebecca asked, pleased that her voice carried no hint of her feelings.

"We're old friends, Bitsy." Again Colleen's voice carried a hint of defiance. "He took it upon himself to let me know he thought I had been unfair to my baby sister . . . to you."

The pounding in Rebecca's heart increased until her chest actually hurt but she ignored it. "Hand me one of those pots, will you?" she asked her sister, pointing to the row of brightly painted clay planters.

Colleen picked up a bright red vessel that was decorated with abstract slashes of blue and yellow. "This one's pretty."

Hiding her automatic smile, Rebecca accepted the pot she had intended to give Colleen for Christmas. "Thanks."

"How can you use that thing?" Colleen asked, pointing to the trowel. "What's it for?"

"It's just for getting a better angle when you're digging. It helps my students overcome their physical limitations." Rebecca had a sudden memory of strong, caring arms circling her and Josh's voice challenging her to approach her conflict with Colleen from a different angle. From her spot on the floor, Rebecca watched Colleen's rigid, defensive posture as she sat back down on the bale of hay. Josh had forced this confrontation without Rebecca's knowledge and clearly without Colleen's enthusiastic support.

With the same slow, gentle movements, Rebecca separated a second calceolaria from the crowded flat and transplanted it into the bright red pot. For a moment, she considered ignoring Josh's hint, but she knew she couldn't go on without some sort of reconciliation with Colleen. When she had watered the newly potted plant, she held it out for Colleen to place on the shelf.

"Come on, Colleen," she teased. "Make yourself useful. Come and help me do this."

Colleen hesitated to kneel down by the plants. "I'll just get the pots for you." She brought two more of the clay pots and set them down beside her sister.

Rebecca nearly lost her temper again, but she caught sight of the trowel and tried another angle. "Don't be afraid. These aren't meat eaters. They won't hurt you."

"I'm not afraid they'll hurt me!" Colleen responded indignantly. "I'm afraid I'll hurt them!"

Rebecca nodded. "I understand, Colleen. But you'll do fine. Come on and help me." She scooted over and made room beside her in front of the flat. "Just take your time." Handing Colleen one of the pots, she showed her how to place a piece of broken pottery in the bottom to allow the water to drain out without taking the soil with it. She let Colleen use the T-handled trowel to scoop her potting soil into her pot.

"Now that you have a nice new home all ready for the plant, you can take it from its old one," Rebecca said.

"How do I do that?"

Rebecca decided not to answer the question directly. "What do you think will happen if you just pull it out?"

Colleen frowned at the flat of crowded plants. The healthy leaves and the fat, round pouchlike blooms looked fairly sturdy, but beneath the soil, the roots looked fragile. "I'm afraid I'll tear off the roots."

Rebecca decided she could afford to sacrifice a few plants in a good cause. "You can try it and see."

Colleen grabbed the stem of the plant beneath the tightly bunched leaves and tried to pull. One of the leaves broke off, but the plant didn't move. She frowned again, and looked questioningly at Rebecca. "It's a stubborn little thing, isn't it?"

Rebecca smiled and lifted her eyebrows but didn't answer.

With a look of grim determination, Colleen grabbed the plant with both hands and pulled hard. After a few seconds of resistance, the stem separated from the root mass, breaking free and sending Colleen backward onto the ground. She held the broken stalk, a few sagging leaves, and the speckled pouch blossoms, but the soil held the life-sustaining roots.

"Oh, Bitsy, I'm so sorry! I told you I couldn't do this. You shouldn't have let me ruin your plant!" Colleen recoiled from the mess, dropping the stalk from her hand and scooting away from the flat. She held unreleased tears and her face flushed nearly as red as the bright clay pot.

Rebecca extended a comforting hand and halted her sister's retreat. "Wait, Colleen. It's okay. It's really okay." She waited until Colleen took a deep breath before continuing. "I have plenty of plants. I like to let my students learn by experimenting. It's okay." With the trowel, she dug out the root mass and shook free the dirt that clung to it. "Just remember, ripping a plant out like that can be just as hard on the soil as it is on the plant."

One tear broke free and slid silently down Colleen's cheek. "I came out here to try to make up with you, Bitsy. Not to make you madder."

Rebecca nodded. "I know that. You haven't made me mad. Now come on and learn how to do this the right way." With gentle fingers she loosened the soil around the roots of the next calceolaria and carefully lifted until the plant and the soil released each other. Then she eased the plant into its new home. "Now you try it."

This time, Colleen worked patiently, but when she began to lift the plant, the slightest resistance frightened her and she quit pulling. "I'm going to break it again!" she cried.

"No you're not," Rebecca assured her. "When the plant is really ready, you can take it out without danger.'' She repositioned Colleen's hand until the leaves and stem rested easily in the palm of her hand and the roots trailed below her fingers. ''Now use your other hand to keep the soil loose and pull up gently.'' The calceolaria lifted easily, and Colleen transferred it to its new pot.

''I did it,'' Colleen said with satisfaction, patting the pot with her grimy fingers. ''I can't believe I did it.''

''You have all sorts of hidden talents.'' Rebecca laughed. ''Now help me do the rest of these.''

They worked in near silence, only speaking about the work and the plants. After they had completed all of the transfers and cleaned up, they walked back to the house together more friendly than they had been in many months. Just as they reached the back door, Colleen stopped and touched Rebecca's arm.

''I may not be as brilliant as you are, Bitsy, but the symbolism isn't lost on me.''

Rebecca didn't answer. She couldn't trust herself to speak.

Colleen sighed and then continued. ''I know you think I yanked Patty away just like I did that plant. I know that.''

Still Rebecca kept silent, but she willed her sister to go on.

''I'm not any better with Patty than I am with those stupid plants, Bitsy!'' Colleen's frustration and despair came flowing out with the words. ''I just don't know how to take care of her.''

Finally Rebecca knew what to say. ''But, Colleen, you did fine with the plants. All you needed was some help. You can learn. You can get better with practice.''

Colleen shook her head. ''No, I can't! I've tried for

six years without making it work. I don't think I can go through with it again. Those people in Cambridge are experts. They're trying to teach her to talk and take care of herself. They have a staff that works with her around the clock. I can't be that consistent with her and have anything left at all to give to Chuck and Shelly.''

Rebecca wanted to argue again. She felt all the old anger and hurt come rushing out, but she knew it wouldn't do anything more than cause another rift with Colleen. With a tremendous effort she held her tongue, and surprisingly Colleen added some of the words that Rebecca wanted to hear.

''And don't think I didn't get the part about the soil. I know you miss her. I also know that you're better off without her. She took all your free time, and she isn't even your child.'' Colleen took a breath. ''But I know I owe you an apology for trying to take her away without giving you a chance to say good-bye. I didn't want a scene. And I figured both of you would be better off if I just took her. Josh really tore into me about that, and I guess he's right. He said I have to quit treating you like you're a child.''

Rebecca bit back a sarcastic retort about the pot calling the kettle black and limited herself to saying, ''I would certainly appreciate it if you would.''

''Yeah. Well, I'm going to go see Patty on Monday, and if you want to go with me you can.''

''I'd love it.'' Rebecca felt a tiny release of the coil that wound so tightly around her heart. ''I would really love it.''

When they entered the kitchen, Josh was holding the Department of Motor Vehicles pamphlet above his head while Caitlin jumped for it. Lindsey shouted in frustration at Amanda and Susan who were home from college for Christmas break and had left their suitcases strewn around the bedroom. Lauren and Kelly were just coming in the front door with their husbands Tim and Rich, and Faye was on the phone with Denise making final plans for Christmas dinner on Wednesday. Bob was probably hiding out on his tractor somewhere.

Colleen shot Rebecca a wry grin and shrugged. "Everything looks pretty normal here."

"Yeah. This family's root ball is getting way too big for the pot."

Chapter Ten

The image of pot-bound roots stayed with Rebecca over the rest of the weekend as the house became even more crowded. Amanda, now a senior in college and recently engaged, brought her fiancé for Sunday dinner, and in honor of the occasion Denise, Mike, their three boys, Colleen, Chuck, and Shelly all squeezed into the house with the rest of the family. Rebecca thought that Josh displayed extreme wisdom by declining an invitation to join them.

"You could come and have dinner with me," he suggested to Rebecca as the entire tribe left church after the Sunday morning service. "I don't think anyone would even notice if you were gone."

Rebecca shot him an unreadable look before she laughed and said, "They'd notice when it came time to wash the dishes!"

He reached for her hands and pulled her toward him

a little, willing her to remain behind while the others walked on to their various vehicles. "Come on," he teased her gently. "We could cook hot dogs in my fireplace."

A few flakes of snow drifted out of the ever-gray sky, landing in his hair and shining there for a few seconds before they melted into tiny damp spots. Rebecca felt herself detaching from the moment, losing once again the touch of closeness with him that seemed so elusive these days.

"I don't like hot dogs," she reminded him. "I really need to go home. I'm going to Cambridge with Colleen tomorrow, and I need to help Mom with some Christmas preparations before I go."

"Things are better with Colleen." It wasn't a question.

"I should thank you for that, I suppose." She withdrew even more.

Josh gripped her hands more tightly. "I didn't do anything, and you know it. I just got the ball rolling a bit. If you hadn't worked things out with her, nothing would have changed."

"She said you told her to stop treating me like a child."

Josh grinned at the memory. "Well, yeah. I did say that."

Pulling her hands away, Rebecca murmured something he couldn't hear.

"What?"

"I said, you should take your own advice. Stop treating me like a child."

"Rebecca, what do you mean?"

"You shouldn't have interfered. I'm glad things are going better between Colleen and me, but you shouldn't have interfered. I'm not a child who needs her big brother to protect her.''

''I didn't say you were.'' He spoke quietly. ''That's not what I was doing.'' He reached for her hands again but she held them behind her back.

''That's what it feels like,'' she answered.

John and Mary Mason stood at their own car, watching the scene between their son and Rebecca Traynor. Josh watched them in turn, watched them arguing with each other and finally climbing into their automobile with shaking heads. They would be arguing about him.

''Maybe you're right. Maybe I was trying to protect you. But maybe it's time you settle things with your family. Maybe it's even time you grew up and got away from them a little.''

''Maybe that's not what I want,'' she retorted, and turning away, she left him there.

Josh watched her walk away with a familiar sinking feeling. Was he going to lose her again? How could they ever work things out if they never had time to themselves, if Rebecca couldn't feel resolved about her family, if Josh couldn't quit trying to protect her from them? Jamming his hands into his jacket pockets, he stared across the parking lot long after she climbed into the family van and it pulled away.

The drive into the hills near Cambridge took two hours and Colleen spent the entire time describing Patty's treatment.

''It's a kind of behavior modification that forces her to pay attention to the therapist and to learn to communicate properly. They don't let her get lost in her counting and sorting rituals.''

"Hmm." Rebecca listened through the description of Patty's rigidly controlled day with mixed feelings. Finally she asked, "Doesn't Patty ever get to do what she wants?"

"But, Rebecca, what Patty wants isn't normal!"

Rebecca didn't want to argue, so she let it go. This was too confusing and complex an issue for her to insist on her way of doing things, but she would try to learn as much as possible while she was here. When they pulled into the long drive of the beautifully land-scaped grounds, she felt her spirits lift. At least the place showed evidence that someone valued the passive benefits of aesthetically arranged plants. Maybe they let the children work in the garden during the warm months.

The director greeted them and led them through the halls of the mock Tudor style building. The dark wood, thick carpets, and comfortable furniture welcomed the many adults who sat reading or talking softly as they waited for their children to finish with their classes. Opening one of the doors, the director stepped back to allow them to enter a classroom.

The room appeared to be nearly identical to the classroom in Patty's school back in Delaware, with the exception of each of the four children being attended individually by an adult. When Colleen and Rebecca entered the room, the adults all looked at them, but Rebecca noticed that none of the children responded. Patty's tutor spoke to her and caught her attention with a snap of her fingers.

"Patty, your mommy is here. Come and say hello to your mommy."

Patty obediently followed the woman toward Colleen and stopped when the woman stopped.

"I'm Miss Franks, Patty's teacher. Greet your mommy, Patty."

"Hello, Mommy," Patty said, looking at the ceiling.

"Go, on, Patty. How do you greet your mommy?"

"Hello, Mommy," Patty repeated, and she reached her hand out to Colleen.

Colleen grabbed Patty's hand, knelt down, and pulled Patty toward her in a hug. "Oh, Patty, I have missed you so much!"

"Hello, Mommy," Patty repeated again. She remained stiff, but she didn't pull away. She kept her eyes on the ceiling most of the time, but she also scanned quickly around the group.

Rebecca watched with trepidation as Colleen continued to hold Patty tightly. Generally, such prolonged contact would upset Patty profoundly, but she seemed to be tolerating it today. Eventually, the director tapped Colleen on the shoulder, and she released her daughter.

"I can't believe it!" Colleen exclaimed. "She's already so much better."

Miss Franks moved back toward the worktable with Patty while Colleen spoke with the director and Rebecca followed her niece. Patty sat back in her former position and reached for a stack of multicolored buttons, but the tutor placed her hand over the buttons and spoke.

"Hold out your hand, Patty."

Patty reached for the buttons again, and again the tutor withheld them.

"Hold out your hand, Patty."

"Hand Patty," Patty replied, and this time she stuck her hand out toward Miss Franks, who shook it.

"Good, Patty." The tutor pushed a button toward Patty.

"One." Patty dropped her hand and reached for another button.

"Shake my hand, Patty," Miss Franks said as she covered the buttons with one hand and held the other out for Patty to reach for and shake.

Eventually Patty lightly touched the teacher's hand, received another button, and counted "two."

Rebecca watched while Colleen and the director reviewed each of the improvements Patty had made during the past week, and what her goals would be for the next week. Colleen and Chuck had decided that Patty would remain at the Cambridge school instead of coming home for Christmas, but they had sent a number of presents for their daughter. With half her attention on Patty, and half on the director, Rebecca listened to the arrangements about the gifts.

"We will allow her to have anything that does not encourage her compulsive counting as long as it doesn't interfere with her training ..." The words faded as Rebecca thought of the occasional hint of softness that she saw on her niece's face when she counted her seeds. Patty didn't seem unhappy here, but she also didn't have any of the softness that Rebecca had come to cherish.

"I brought a planting box that Patty used to enjoy. Will she be able to keep it?" Rebecca interrupted the director to ask.

"Planting box?"

"She used to help me garden, and I made a portable box that she could take with her to play in the dirt. She was ready to start growing some seedlings."

The director's face lit up with the first genuine smile

Rebecca had seen in this place. "You must be Bitsy!"

Colleen and Rebecca both stepped back with surprise at this outburst.

"Yes, I'm her aunt. She calls me Bitsy."

"We encourage the children to spend time in the greenhouse every day. Many of them resist it at first, because it is so strange to them, but Patty seemed to know her way around. She actually began to speak there spontaneously, and she kept repeating the name 'Bitsy.' She clearly makes a connection between you and the plants."

"Yes. She would." Rebecca felt a glow spreading from her heart like heat radiating out to thaw parts of herself that had been frozen since Patty left. "I'm glad she made the connection. That seems significant."

"Her spontaneous speech and action are even more significant, but she does have a tendency to drift into counting while she's in the greenhouse."

Colleen watched Patty working with the tutor and the buttons, reaching out to touch the woman in return for the reward of one more button to count. They remained in the classroom for some time, watching the progress; and with Rebecca's urging, Colleen even joined in Patty's lesson while Rebecca returned to the car for the presents. When Colleen held out her hand she received a light touch in exchange for a button.

"Seven. Seven green, twelve blue, two white, three brown," Patty proclaimed in her flat voice when the lesson ended and Miss Franks scooped the buttons back into a plastic jar.

"I don't understand why this is different from the other kinds of counting she does," Colleen commented.

"Because we're using it to encourage her to develop normal skills,'' the tutor replied. ''It's highly motivating for her, so we use it.''

''But . . .'' Colleen didn't know what she wanted to say, she just knew that something bothered her about the process.

''It's not anything different from what you've tried yourself, Mrs. Weaver. We're just much more consistent. We do this around the clock and for every behavior. Eventually, it will allow Patty to act more like other people.''

''Yes. I understand.'' Colleen nodded in agreement.

Rebecca returned to the room carrying Patty's dirt box. ''Look what I have for you, Patty.''

''Dirt,'' Patty said.

Miss Franks watched with some astonishment as Patty walked to the box, opened the lid, and began scooping dirt with her tiny trowel.

''Micky hand feet. Two hundred twenty-seven seeds. Seven green, twelve blue, two white, three brown. Micky Buckeye.'' Patty began remembering the day in the barn, and Rebecca knelt down beside her. Compared with her normal speech, this avalanche of words surprised even Rebecca.

''That's right, Patty. Remember the fun we had that day?''

''Micky Buckeye. Two hundred twenty-seven seeds. Seven green, twelve blue, two white, three brown. Josh Blackeye.''

Rebecca gasped. Then she laughed a great, joyous laugh. She wanted Patty to know that she understood her joke. ''Oh, Patty! That's right! Micky Buckeye! Josh Blackeye! And it was all my fault that poor Josh got a black eye. You are a very funny girl, Patty. And I love you.''

"Funny girl, Patty," Patty said without any inflection as she continued to dig in her box of dirt. Without shifting her concentration from the box, Patty lifted her free hand and lightly grabbed Rebecca's finger. Slowly her upper body shifted until her head barely touched Rebecca's arm. She pulled out another bulb from the box. "Three."

Colleen signed a release after Miss Franks and the school's administrator both agreed that Rebecca should be allowed to visit Patty any time she wanted, but the drive back to Delaware was tense with the strain that began with Patty's reaction to Rebecca. By the time the sisters hit the I-270 outer belt around Columbus and headed north toward Delaware, Rebecca couldn't stand the silence any longer.

"Colleen, you have to understand that she has spent a lot of time with me, and it has been important time. She was developing a lot. I tried to tell you before, but you wouldn't listen."

"I understand that she can do things with you that she can't do with me." Colleen spoke angrily. "You might have made her be willing to touch you, but those people are trying to get her to touch *me*. They understand that *I* am her mother."

Rebecca watched out the window as the traffic slowed to its normal late-afternoon gridlock. "I don't want to be her mother, Colleen. But I do love her. Why wouldn't you want me to love her? I love Micky, Robbie, and Danny, too. I would probably love Shelly, except that you never bring her around. You keep her at home with Chuck as if you're trying to hoard them." She clamped her mouth shut to keep from saying anything else.

"But I want Patty to love *me!* Don't you understand that?" Colleen slammed on the brakes as she crept too close to a stopped car. "Sorry. This probably isn't the time to discuss this."

"It may be our best time. We're stuck here and neither of us can run away from it," Rebecca countered. "I want Patty to love you, too. That's why I don't understand how you could send her to live somewhere else."

"I told you why. I love her, but I can't handle her."

"Okay, I don't want to argue about it anymore," Rebecca temporized. "But I want you to consider something. I just want you to think about it. Don't give me an answer yet."

"What?"

"Okay. I watched that Miss Franks today. Now, I know that those people are specially trained, and that they have a big enough staff to watch those kids all day, but I don't think they are really doing anything different from what we have been doing. The difference is that at home, sometimes Patty gets to relax. She gets some time off just to be autistic."

"What do you mean? She's always autistic."

"I mean that we all expect Patty to fit into our world. She's supposed to adjust to us. She's supposed to learn how to communicate with us and be 'normal.' "

"Of course. That's the way the world is, Rebecca. It won't do her any good in life for me to become autistic like her. Then we'd just both be sunk."

"I know that. But I'm saying that at least some of the time, we need to try to look at things from her perspective. If her counting is a relief for her, why

shouldn't she get to do it sometimes? And why should
it always be held out of her control?''

''Because she gets lost in there. I'll never reach her
if she goes away inside her head completely.''

''But look at what happened today. She made contact with me. She just did it in her own way. We met
somewhere in the middle.''

''What are you suggesting?''

''Think about letting her come back. I could show
you the things I did with her in the greenhouse and
you could do those things with her yourself. We could
work with the teacher in the Delaware school. She
could still live out at the farm.''

''No.''

''Just think about it.''

''I mean she can't live at the farm anymore.''

''Why not?''

Colleen inched the car along and looked at the clock
on the dashboard. ''We're never going to get home.''

''Why won't you let her live at the farm anymore?''

''Because Dad said she can't.''

''What!'' Rebecca felt an entirely new brand of betrayal. ''I can't believe it!''

''He's right, Rebecca. He said I was taking advantage of you, and that you have your own life to live
now. Dad says you haven't been out on a date in over
a year. He says you can't be expected to watch Patty
all the time.''

''He's a fine one to talk!'' Rebecca could feel her
temper rising. ''He'd keep me home cooking his dinner and washing his dishes forever, if he didn't know
Mom would object. Anyway, why can't we all help
out? What good is it having eight sisters if we can't
help one another out with the hard stuff?''

"But Patty is my responsibility. Not yours. Not anyone else's. She's mine."

"What about Chuck? Isn't she his responsibility, too? And can't the rest of us take on some responsibility if we want to? Isn't that what family is all about? We're all in this child-raising business together. What's that African saying? 'It takes an entire village to raise a child.' And that's a child without special problems."

Colleen's laugh brought Rebecca's diatribe to a close. "Rebecca, you can get down off your soapbox now. I'll think about it. I promise. I don't promise I'll agree with you, but I'll talk to Chuck, and we'll think about it."

Chapter Eleven

Colleen passed off the outer belt and onto Route 23 and within a few minutes the traffic broke. Rebecca relaxed with a sigh as the two sisters moved steadily home through the early evening darkness. Taillights lurched a little unsteadily in front of them as Colleen swung onto the county road behind a vehicle that they recognized was Josh's truck.

"You don't think he's been drinking, do you?" Colleen asked in horror. "Surely not Josh. He's always been so straight."

Rebecca laughed. "I think it's more likely that Caitlin is driving. She was supposed to get her temporary license today, and he probably took her out on the road."

"Yeah. You're probably right. That boy sure needs to settle down and have his own family. He's been hanging around taking care of my little sisters forever.

146

He taught you how to drive, too," Colleen realized in amazement. "Rebecca, do you remember when he used to come around and perk you up? You were always trailing after him. He was so nice about it. I don't think he ever told you to get lost. He's just a natural with stray animals and stray kids."

Rebecca watched the taillights in silence until Colleen turned to examine her face.

"What is it, Rebecca?"

"Colleen, do you realize that you have been calling me Rebecca all day? In fact, you started it the other day. What happened? I've been complaining about being 'Bitsy' for years without anyone paying me the least bit of attention."

Colleen followed the truck into the Traynors' drive and shut off the engine before she answered. "You're right. I hadn't thought about it, but with Josh always being so formal and calling you Rebecca it just didn't seem right to call you 'Bitsy.' I suppose I see you more as an adult now."

Caitlin pounded on the outside of Colleen's window and shouted, "Did you see? Did you see me? I drove all the way to Lewis Center and back. Josh says I'll be ready to take the road test soon!" Her brilliant blond hair swung back and forth as she looked from one sister to the other. "Isn't he the best?" Caitlin squeezed Rebecca with a quick hug. "And he's so cute! I can't believe he's willing to spend all this time teaching me how to drive," she whispered before rushing into the house.

Josh had been leaning against the truck watching the scene with a tolerant smile. Now he sauntered over, hands shoved into his jeans pockets, kicking a rock with the toe of his shoe. Rebecca and Colleen looked so relaxed with each other that he couldn't prevent the satisfied grin that spread across his face. His prospects for the evening suddenly seemed a whole lot brighter.

"If you say 'aw, shucks, ma'am, t'weren't nothin','" I promise I'll go get my pa's shotgun and chase you off this land!" Rebecca warned him with a glare. "You look disgustingly pleased with yourself."

Colleen thought she caught a glint of something in Josh's eye that was a far cry from "aw, shucks" and she had a sudden, shattering insight into the dynamics between these two. With a swallow of her sisterly desire to tease, she decided that a quick exit might be in order. "Uh, I'll see you two later . . . I've got to go help Mom . . . I'll tell her you'll be in in a minute . . . okay?"

"No." Josh didn't look at Colleen, and it wasn't clear what his negative meant.

"No?" she asked.

Rebecca folded her arms across her chest and continued to glare, but something in Josh's steady approach sent a wave of confusion through her.

He kept walking straight toward Rebecca as Colleen sidestepped toward the house. "You can tell your mom that Rebecca and I won't be here for dinner tonight," he said, smiling wickedly without taking his eyes off Rebecca.

"Now wait a minute," Rebecca objected. "Mom's got a house full of people. She's going to need my help."

"Go on, Colleen," Josh said mildly. "Your mom's got a house full of people who are perfectly capable of helping themselves. Rebecca and I are going someplace else."

"Got it," Colleen agreed and practically raced toward the house. She had experienced Josh Mason's temper once this week already, and she wasn't about to test it a second time.

Rebecca, on the other hand, seemed more than ready for a good fight. Although things seemed to be improving with Colleen, the day had been long and stressful, and Rebecca had just about used up all her emotional control. On top of that, she had been working so many hours lately that she hadn't finished any of her Christmas plans other than the pots for her sisters. Tomorrow was Christmas Eve, and Rebecca hadn't even felt the season arrive.

But the worst, most aggravating problem of all stood about a foot away from her now. Since that one afternoon at the pond, Josh had reverted to his old, familiar way of treating her as if he were an older brother and as if she were what Colleen called a "stray kid." She had had enough of his high-handed interfering with her relationships, and his telling her where she would eat, and his barging into the family meals as if he belonged there, and his teaching her little sister how to drive, and his coming out to check on her marshland project every step of the way, and his holding her when she cried for Patty but never doing anything more than kissing her on the top of her head as if she were a little child, and his . . .

Rebecca didn't know when her thoughts had become words or when her words had become action; she only knew that she found herself running away from Josh as fast as she could, out into the fields. She only knew that she wanted to release a terrible, pent-up energy somehow and this way seemed to be working until she heard a muffled grunt followed by a groan and a "Wait up, will you? For Pete's sake, Rebecca, slow down a little." Josh sounded exasperated. "I thought all you therapists were supposed to be able to face your problems."

"No," she answered, taking a perverse delight in sounding as determined as he had a few minutes earlier, and starting off into a run again.

"Okay. You asked for it." He suddenly caught up to her and grabbed her hands. She started to squeak a protest, but no sound came out as Josh pulled her against his chest with a bear hug of considerable strength. For a minute she thought she might suffocate.

"Are you going to stop running away?" His voice came to her through layers of down jackets and stocking caps.

Rebecca nodded.

"Say it."

"I won't run away."

"Very good. Now, I'm going to let you go, but don't even think about escaping again. Got it?"

"I'm not escaping anything. What do you mean, escape? How dare you!"

Josh held her pinned immobile against his chest while her protests continued in a muffled litany of complaints. Finally she ran out of steam and held herself still while her anger seeped away into embarrassment.

"Do you promise not to run away anymore?" he asked softly.

"Yes. I promise," she sulked. "I'm sorry. I didn't mean to."

Immediately he dropped his arms and stepped away from her.

"That's much better." Josh smiled. "Let's go."

"I need to go inside first," Rebecca protested. "I haven't been home all day. I'm sure Mom needs my help."

"No she doesn't, Rebecca. She already knows we're going out to dinner. I told her. Now let's go."

"You . . ."

"Don't start again. Let's get out of here before someone comes looking for you."

It seemed like such a small thing, but it was so very difficult: just to leave, to walk away and take an evening for herself when she might be needed at home. She almost couldn't do it. He watched her ambivalence, watched her fight with this need to be in the center of her family, and he sent up a quick prayer that her desire to be with him would be stronger. They were wonderful people and he loved them, but for once he wished she would freely choose him.

Rebecca stood looking at the warm glow of lamplight beckoning from the windows. She heard a peal of laughter floating out of the closed windows and a light went out upstairs. The shadows behind the living room curtains indicated people moving toward the dining room and she knew they were all gathering at the table. Someone else would be carrying in the platters of food and glasses of milk. Panic started in her stomach and rose to her chest and throat. Would they even know she was missing?

"Rebecca." Josh stood several feet away from her, his face hidden in the shadowy night. He didn't go on until she dragged her eyes away from the house and back toward him. "I can't force you away from them, but I would really like to take you out for dinner. Do you want to eat with me?"

With a little dip of her head she answered tentatively, "Sure. I want to eat with you. I just don't see why we can't stay here."

He moved closer then and took her hand. "Because I want you to myself for once." The glint in his eye that she had seen earlier returned now, oddly shining even stronger as the night darkness deepened. "I don't want to share you with a dozen other people. I want you to learn how to go on a date."

For the briefest moment she let herself feel warm, wanted, desirable. He wanted her to be alone with him on a date. A date. The odd phrasing of his sentence stuck in her head. He wanted her to learn *how* to go on a date. He sounded like her father.

The feelings of betrayal came flooding back. How could she have been sidetracked even for a minute from her need to get Patty back home? Her parents had banished Patty because they wanted Rebecca to go out on dates! They had never cared about her social life before. They had never worried about her spending too much time taking care of her niece or nephews. Why would they suddenly tell Colleen that Patty had to stay away? She had a picture memory of her father and Josh disappearing into the living room to discuss "what you're teaching my daughter."

"You!" The word gushed from her as if she had been punched in the stomach, and she stared at Josh with the realization of what he had said. He wanted to teach her how to date. It was one more of those lessons he thought she ought to learn, like how to drive and how to incubate quail chicks. Her father had always been contented to let her stay at home and take care of things, but not Josh. Josh wanted her to learn about life.

The lesson he had always tried most strenuously to

teach her was the one about getting some independence from her family. He didn't want to share her with her family, he wanted to force her to get away from them. He had always tried to protect her from her own family, had told her she needed to separate from them and have her own life. He had always tried to take care of her life.

Josh had manipulated Colleen into reconciliation, he had manipulated her father into letting him teach Caitlin to drive (a task that would have fallen to Rebecca since her father never would have had the time), and he had even managed to get them to start using her real name. Josh must be the one responsible for her parents' sudden decision not to keep Patty on the farm. Like some nineteenth-century *padrone*, he must have decided that Rebecca should start dating. He didn't want her himself, and now he didn't want her to have Patty. He wanted her to go out and have the life he thought she should have. All for Rebecca's own good, of course.

Everything went numb. For a few seconds, she felt dead. She wondered briefly if a person could simply stop all those autonomic functions because the world seemed too bleak a place to continue living.

"Rebecca. What's wrong?" Josh watched in confusion as Rebecca's face showed first the temptation of going on the date, then a kind of awakening horror followed by the ultimate withdrawal. He almost wished he hadn't stopped her from running away. The pain of seeing her flee couldn't begin to compare with what he felt now.

Her heart had resumed its beating, but it thudded with a limp, as if it had been so seriously bruised that each contraction reinjured it and spread the pain fur-

ther. When she heard Josh step closer to her, she retreated. She couldn't bear this. She couldn't bear being
close to him, feeling the draw of his presence and
knowing that he was responsible for her loss.

"Rebecca?"

"No." She managed to release the word and take
another step away from him. The distance helped a
little. "No."

"What's wrong?" Josh asked again. Something had
gone terribly wrong with this silly plan of his to kid-
nap her for dinner. He moved toward her again, but
her immediate jerk backward shocked him into
immobility.

"Go away." It was the only thing she could think
of to say. "Please just go away."

"I . . ." he started, and stopped in frustration. "As
soon as you tell me what's wrong."

"Go away," she repeated. She knew she couldn't
last much longer if she had to continue speaking, so
she closed her mouth and stared into the distance.

The pain in his gut suddenly boiled into anger. If
she could lose her temper, then so could he. "Fine.
You don't want to talk about whatever demon just
crawled up your spine, then don't. But don't give me
that garbage about how you're just not wired to share
your feelings, Rebecca!" He heard the temper in his
voice and became even angrier that he could lose control of himself this way. He shouted, "If you don't
want to be treated like a child then quit acting like
one!"

Unfortunately, his temper failed to reach her. Wrap-
ping her arms around herself, Rebecca stared into the
distance and held herself contained within an impen-
etrable wall of numbness. With something close to a

growl, Josh opened the door and climbed into the truck. "Let me know when you're ready to talk about it!"

For the first time in his life, Josh spun his tires and spit gravel in an effort to race away from his own feelings. For the first time in his life, he didn't feel the need to protect Rebecca Traynor from those feelings; but for the first time in his life, he seriously doubted that he had the power ever to capture Rebecca Traynor's love.

Rebecca clung to her paralysis because the alternative seemed to be flying into a million pieces and blowing away into the freezing night air, but eventually the bruising in her heart traveled to her legs and she sank into a painful crouch. She was still there, hunched over herself, when Faye came to pull her up and guide her back into the house.

"What have you and that boy managed to do to each other now, Little Bit?" her mother grumbled gently as she pushed her daughter into bed. "You're the two most obstinate creatures ever put on the face of the earth. I don't know why you can't just face up to the truth and get on with your lives."

She waited for a response from her daughter, but Rebecca only turned over, curled into a ball, and closed her eyes.

Chapter Twelve

"She doesn't want to talk to me, Dad, and I'm not going to go crawling back apologizing for something I don't even understand," Josh argued as he swung the long-handled ax down into the sawed end of a thick pine log. Lifting the log and ax together, he smashed them into the chopping stump and split the wood into two pieces. With a well-practiced motion he tossed the pieces onto a large pile and hefted another log onto the chopping block.

"Seems to me you've both got about as much sense as that stick of wood," John Mason replied as he stacked the split wood neatly beside his house. "It seems like a terrible thing that you would spend Christmas snarling at each other instead of being kind to each other." He had been shocked after the Christmas Eve service last night to hear Rebecca and Josh sniping at each other while the rest of the congregation

156

milled around expressing pleasant wishes for Christmas.

"Look, Dad." Josh sighed as he tossed two more helpings of firewood on the pile. "I've been sweet and careful to that woman all her life. I've walked on eggshells whenever there was the least chance that I might hurt her. I never pressured her, I never told her how I felt, I've never been anything but a fool Boy Scout where she's concerned. It seems to me it's time I started watching out for my own feelings."

"Well, then?" John pulled out a handkerchief and wiped his balding forehead. In spite of the Christmas chill, the hard labor had dampened his flannel shirt and jeans. Josh dripped sweat as if he had just stepped out of a shower, and his hands showed signs of blistering over his calluses.

"Well then, what?" Josh grunted, fighting through a particularly large knot in the log before him.

"Well then, why don't you tell the girl how you feel instead of wearing both of us out by splitting more firewood than I'll need for two winters?" John watched Josh lever the ax from the wood to try again against the knot and threw both his hands up in despair. "Look at you. You're the most stubborn-headed ox I've ever known. Leave the wood alone and go talk to Rebecca."

In frustration Josh slammed the ax into the log one more time. The iron resistance of the knot failed to give way, and the resulting jolt sent a spasm of pain through Josh's wrists into his shoulders. "Ahh . . ." He cut off the curse before he began it.

John stepped forward and rubbed his son's shoulder just as if he didn't have to stretch up to reach it.

"Come inside. How did I ever manage to raise a son with such wretchedly strong self-control?"

Josh snorted. "That part is all your fault. You're the one who told me to be careful. You must have told me a thousand times to watch out around Rebecca. Well, it looks like I watched myself right out of her life."

They scraped mud off their boots before entering the house, anticipating the lecture they would receive otherwise, and then stood facing each other as if waiting for some miracle of understanding to descend on them. Finally Josh shrugged and started toward the kitchen.

"Want some coffee?" he asked his dad, lifting the pot off the burner.

"Son, that was a long time ago."

"Yeah, want some coffee?" He knew exactly how long ago it had been.

"I didn't expect your feelings to last so long."

"Well, they did. Do you want any coffee or not?"

"Josh, she's an adult now. Five years' difference doesn't mean a thing at your age."

Shoving the coffeepot back with a gesture of frustration, Josh squared his shoulders and turned to face his father directly. "You know what, Dad? With Rebecca and me, five years' difference never meant a thing. Never. Get your own coffee; I'm not fit company today." He stormed to the front door, but John stopped him with his words.

"Josh, I love you. And Bob Traynor loves his daughter. Neither of us ever wanted to cause you hurt, but we didn't want you two hurting yourselves, either. It wasn't right before." He took a deep breath and plunged on into the painful truth. "If it's not right now, I'm sorry. But I wasn't wrong back then."

Josh held himself tightly still and let the feelings of pain and disappointment settle in his heart before he nodded. "You're right. And maybe 'now' doesn't have anything to do with 'then.' Maybe it just isn't right 'now.'" He let himself out of his parents' home, and sped off into the cold December night wondering if it would ever be right.

John Mason spun around at the touch of his wife's hand on his shoulder. He lifted her fingers to his lips and apologized. "I'm sorry, Mary. I'm afraid I just made him angrier. I didn't mean to run him off on Christmas Day."

To his surprise Mary smiled a soft little smile and answered, "Don't fret. He'll be all right. They have to learn how to fight with each other sometime. He can't spend the rest of his life holding his breath because he's afraid of hurting her. Rebecca Traynor is a strong-minded woman, and Josh is a strong-minded man. Now they'll either learn how to pull together to work things out . . . or they won't."

"What will happen to him if they don't?"

Mary snorted impatiently. "He'll survive. People survive loss all the time. I know he loves her, but he won't die if she doesn't love him back."

"He's loved her for an awfully long time," John reminded her with a sense of guilt.

"Yes, well, if he loses her, he'll hurt for an awfully long time," Mary answered, ignoring the sadness in her own heart for this amazing son of hers.

Three weeks later, Rebecca and Josh forged their way carefully around the slick sides of the partially frozen pond. The frigid air was balmy compared to their relationship, but they had work to do, and they were both too professional to let their emotions interfere with it. Neither of them had spoken about what had happened two days before Christmas, and they had successfully avoided being alone together until today. If their public conversations contained painful sarcasm, few besides themselves could recognize it.

Josh continued to instruct Caitlin in the finer points of handling a truck, but he showed up after dinner, took her out for half an hour, and dropped her off again without coming into the house. When Bob asked Rebecca what had happened, she answered angrily that apparently someone had formed the ridiculous notion that she wanted to date. She hoped she had finally put that rumor to rest, and that people would stop attempting to manipulate her life for her. Bob sputtered for a few minutes until Faye quietly told him to leave it be.

In spite of the bad weather, Rebecca and Colleen managed to travel to Cambridge every week, and with the horticultural therapy as a common activity they seemed to be bonding with each other as well as Patty. They spent time together in the school's greenhouse, and Colleen at last began to relax around her daughter. They even found themselves laughing together occasionally. Patty's language skills continued to improve slightly, and Colleen seriously considered bringing her daughter back home by summer. But Colleen remained adamant that Patty would not return to the farm, and Rebecca held on to her unspoken fury with Josh.

When Josh had arrived at the farm to drive Rebecca to gather and plant the willows, she had insisted that she could drive herself. With cold indignation she informed him that she had received her driver's permit nine years earlier, that she had registered to vote seven years earlier, that she had received her bachelor's degree three years earlier, and that she had owned her own business for a year and a half. Josh had bitingly remarked that it was too bad she hadn't bothered to grow up somewhere during all that time, since an adult would understand the conservation involved in using one vehicle rather than two. Rebecca swung herself up into his truck and slammed the door—forcefully.

Now she trudged silently beside him through an icy drizzle of January rain, yoked by their mutual stewardship of this plot of land. Earlier in the day they had taken cuttings from the mature willows in Grove Marsh, and Rebecca wanted to get them planted quickly. She and Josh each carried a short crowbar, a hammer, and a canvas bag full of what appeared to be foot-long, pointed sticks. Ice thinly crusted the shallow water, crackling and shattering whenever their boots slid too far down the slippery bank.

"You start here and I'll go on down to the far end to start," Rebecca suggested. "We'll meet in the middle."

"Fine," Josh replied as he pulled one of the willow spikes from his bag. He watched her foot dip a little deeper into the freezing water. "Don't get too wet. It's cold enough for frostbite."

"I can take care of myself," she answered, dropping the temperature a few more degrees as she walked away.

"I never doubted it!" he remarked through gritted teeth. He watched her a few minutes longer, simply enjoying the way she swung the tools and bag, then kicked himself for prolonging his torture.

They worked toward each other in silence for an hour: pounding the crowbar down into the mud at the pond's edge, pulling it out to slip the spike into the hole, and then pounding the spike itself down even farther. Using their boots, they then pressed the muddy soil tightly against the cuttings to hold them upright at the water's edge. The necessity of working in the water in the freezing weather cost them energy, and they wasted no effort to speak to each other. The waterproofing of Rebecca's boots could have been better, and she tried to ignore the numbness creeping from her toes to her ankles.

Josh straightened and stretched his back; he had planted all but four of his cuttings and had worked nearly halfway down the length of the pond. The long line of bare sticks didn't look like much. He looked for Rebecca, but couldn't see her.

''Rebecca?''

He heard a small grunt of complaint, realized she was bent over and hidden by a small rise, and started toward her.

''Rats!''

''What's wrong?'' he called.

''My boot sunk so deep in the mud that I can't pull it out and there's nothing to hold onto for leverage.''

''Wait a minute and I'll help you.''

''That's all right. I'll get it in a minute . . . Oh, no . . . oh . . . *oh!*''

Just as Josh crested the rise he saw Rebecca's foot pull completely out of her boot, throwing her off balance. She teetered precariously for a few seconds, weight on her right foot, left foot waving in the air, hammer in one hand, crowbar bobbing in the other. For a brief moment, he thought she would hold the position until she could put her left foot back into her boot, but suddenly the mud bank under her right foot gave way to the hidden muskrat tunnel beneath it. With a little scream, Rebecca toppled like a cut tree, completely submerging in the half-frozen pond.

"Rebecca!" He raced straight into the water, ignoring the frigid liquid seeping into his boots. "Are you all right?" He grabbed her and pulled her out of the pond just as the wind picked up for a hearty blow.

"I d-d-dropped the hammer," she stammered.

"Forget the stupid hammer," he shouted at her, hugging her close as he pulled her back to the shore and getting himself nearly as wet as she.

"I c-c-can't. It's my b-best hammer," she argued, shoving him away and reaching back into the water to try to find the tool.

"Rebecca! Get out of the pond right now!" Josh was becoming very angry with her. "You'll get hypothermic if you don't get out of there and get dry."

She ignored him and walked farther into the pond, nearly fully submerged again as she bent low. Josh followed again and was bracing himself to lift her out by force when she raised her hand high with a triumphant shout. "Here it is!"

He tore the hammer out of her hand, and pulled her back onto dry, or rather muddy, land. "Get back to the truck!" he shouted again. He picked up the remaining tools and pushed her ahead of him back around the way they had come. "Go faster!"

By this time, Rebecca was trying to obey him. She knew she was losing body heat rapidly, but she couldn't move any faster. Her feet were completely numb, her fingers were stiff, her face burned with a sharp, stinging pain. Stumbling at last, she fell into a little heap with a quarter of the distance still to go.

"I'm sorry. I'm sorry." She tried to apologize for

slowing him up, but she couldn't speak properly. Suddenly she felt his strong arms lifting her up and helping her stand again.

"Come on, Rebecca, keep moving." He no longer shouted at her, and his voice sounded gentle in her ear. "Keep moving, sweetheart. We'll make it. We're almost there." And she was moving again, somehow making her frozen muscles carry her to the truck, although she felt sure that she didn't actually carry her own weight. Josh's voice urged her, coddled her, prodded her, until at last he yanked open the door of his truck and lifted her onto the seat.

She started to worry about getting his truck wet until he told her to shut up and let him fasten her seat belt. The motor coughed to life, but by then, Rebecca couldn't hear anything except the rattling of her teeth. Josh pulled a dirty blanket from behind the seat and threw it over her.

"This is better than nothing, but it's not much," he growled. Throwing the truck into gear, he sped out of the parking lot with gravel flying, and prayed he wouldn't be stopped by the cops before he could get her someplace warm and dry. Rebecca's influence on his driving habits was becoming dangerous.

Rebecca huddled into the seat, a lump of frozen mud, and wished the engine would warm up enough for Josh to turn on the heater. She concentrated on making herself as small as possible, trying to conserve whatever body heat she still possessed, and she didn't pay any attention to their direction until Josh stopped the truck and began pulling her out.

"Where are we?" she mumbled through frozen lips.

"My house," he answered shortly, practically carrying her through a small woods and onto the low porch of a modern log cabin. "It's a lot closer than yours."

He fumbled with a key while she continued to shiver, but eventually he got the door opened and she felt the blessed warmth of central heating. Log cabin or not, this was a real house. With a little persuasion, Josh managed to head Rebecca to a plush bathroom where he started hot water in the tub, pulled a couple of bath towels from a cabinet, and pointed to a heavy flannel robe hanging on the door.

"Take a hot bath and put on the robe. If you'll throw out your wet clothes, I'll put them in the laundry."

She was too cold and miserable to argue, and she really didn't want to, so she followed his advice. In a short time, she was sitting bundled in his robe and a blanket in front of a roaring fire drying her hair and drinking a mug of hot chocolate. Even after the bath her toes remained a little numb and she inched closer to the fire.

"What about you?" Rebecca looked guiltily at Josh over the edge of her cup. "You're practically as wet and cold as I was."

"If you're all right, I'll go shower and change now," he conceded. "Make yourself at home. There are plenty of books to look at."

Rebecca nearly smiled as she tried to find any wall space that didn't contain a shelf filled with books. "I'll be fine. Go get warm." Then she stopped him before he could obey. "I didn't know you weren't still living with your parents! I've always thought of you as being at their house in Delaware."

He rolled his eyes at her foolishness. "We're a more independent kind of family than yours. They didn't mind helping support an adult son through graduate school, Rebecca, but I think they were relieved when I finally started earning enough money to get out of their house.''

She grimaced. ''I guess neither of us is as young as we remember.''

He looked at her swallowed up by the blanket and robe, pale and still a little damp, and he thought she looked as young and innocent as the child he used to watch out for. On the other hand, he had to admit she had developed a mind more determined than most other adults he knew, and beneath that robe was the body of a woman. He wondered if she had any idea how hard it was always to pretend he wasn't attracted to her. Suppressing a resurgence of his anger, he left the room, wondering if he would ever take the risk of talking to her about it.

Chapter Thirteen

Rebecca finished her hot chocolate, and finally felt warm enough to wander around the room looking at the bookshelves. She recognized some of the poetry they had read together during Josh's senior year of high school, and the books he had written to her about when he first went away to college. She had missed his letters desperately when he had stopped writing after his sophomore year. Now she looked carefully down the shelf to see what he had read after they lost touch.

The three black canvas volumes didn't have titles, and she pulled them out anticipating a look at Josh's laboratory or field notes, but when she opened the first volume, an envelope slipped out and fell to the floor, landing face up with her own name written in Josh's plain strong script. Rebecca moved sluggishly, tired from her dunking and sleepy from the cozy heat of

167

the room. Without consciously thinking, she carried the books back to her chair and began reading the letter which had apparently been written to her. She didn't even question why it hadn't been sent until she was too engrossed to stop herself.

All the frustration and confusion of an innocent young man whose intentions had been questioned spread across the pages of that letter, blaming first his father, then her sisters, then herself, and finally himself for the necessity of ending their friendship. Apparently everyone he knew had made him feel guilty about forcing his attentions on someone much too young for him, and he apologized even in the midst of his anger. The letter rambled on with his protesting that his feelings were only those of an older brother and friend. Had Josh ever really been as young as this letter sounded? He had always been so wise in her eyes, but this letter came from someone barely out of his own childhood.

She tucked the pages back into the envelope and realized she held not field notes but personal journals. And they were not just journals, but contained information about Josh's most intimate feelings. With a sigh she closed the book, shook her head, and stood to carry them back to the shelf. She wanted to read them more than she had ever wanted anything, but she already felt guilty about seeing the letter.

''There's probably enough humiliating material in there to keep you and your sisters entertained for a couple of years.'' Josh stood at the door to the room. His wet hair dripped onto the towel draped around his bare shoulders and he held a pair of socks for the bare feet that showed beneath his clean pair of blue jeans. His farmer's tan had nearly faded, but she could still see the darkness of the skin on his arms contrasting with the slightly lighter color of his chest. His eyes held hers steadily.

"I'm sorry. I didn't mean to pry. I saw my name on the letter, and I read it before I thought about what I was doing." She couldn't blame the fire for the heat in her face, but she thought it might also be dishonest to say her blush derived entirely from her embarrassment about reading his letter.

"I really don't mind," he insisted. "If I had mailed it to you when I wrote it, we might have figured out a way to stay friends and you wouldn't have been so disappointed in me."

"Why didn't you send it?"

"I think it was pretty self-serving." He shrugged. "I haven't read it in a long time, but if memory serves me, I was awfully young then."

"Too young. Too old. It isn't an easy age for anyone." She smiled, temporarily forgetting her anger with him. "When I was twenty, all I could think about was getting to Florida for spring break."

Josh walked into the room and took the books from her before sitting down in front of the fire. "That's not true. I remember you at twenty."

Rebecca rolled her eyes skeptically and sat back down beside him. "Oh, right. You were long gone by then."

With a lifted eyebrow Josh opened the second volume, flipped through the pages until he found what he wanted, and handed it back to her. "I had grown up a little by then," he commented as he dropped the other books on the floor and leaned over to put on his socks.

She read with astonishment:

Each time I see Rebecca I am struck again with how much love she offers those around her. I watched her in church this morning, helping Denise and Colleen with the two babies, and reassuring her mother about Amanda, Susan, and Lindsey, who had snuck out to the parking lot to talk to the boys there. Little Caitlin is just the age Rebecca was when I first met her, but I don't think Rebecca was ever that young and carefree. She's been taking care of someone every minute I have known her. I wish I could take her off somewhere just to let her play.

"I don't recall you ever making it to Florida for spring break," he stated flatly.

"Josh, where were you?" Rebecca looked at him in confusion.

He stood and picked up her empty cup. "Want some more?"

"I want to understand. I thought you had completely forgotten me at that point in our lives."

He walked to the kitchen with her cup and busied himself with more hot chocolate for both of them. As she watched him through the doorway from her spot on the couch, she wondered if she really saw his hands shaking. He clattered the spoons and cups for a few more minutes, but finally returned to her side and handed her a cup.

"So tell me," she persisted, her irritation showing again. "If you still wanted to be my friend, why didn't you just pick up where we left off? I wasn't a child anymore by then. Your father couldn't have complained that I was too young."

"It wasn't that simple, Rebecca."

"Why not? What wasn't so simple?"

He looked at the volume still in her hand and then searched her face so carefully that she wondered what he sought there. "Maybe the easiest thing would be just to let you read that," he said even as he held his hand out to retrieve the book, "but I'm not sure I'm quite that brave."

"Is it that bad?" She could see that he hurt, but she still didn't understand why. He shivered. "Maybe you should get some more clothes on," she suggested.

"I'm sure I should." He stood up quickly and disappeared into one of the rooms past the kitchen, still carrying the book.

Rebecca reached down and found the other two volumes by the side of the sofa, drawn by her curiosity but fearful of that hurt look in his eyes. She knew her expectations of him were unrealistic, that she thought of him as stronger than the rest of the world, but surely he could have explained to his father that their friendship was a rare and precious thing. What awful secret made it not so simple? And why did it matter anymore?

The fire crackled as the dried wood burned hot and Rebecca snuggled deeper into the large robe. It carried Josh's scent, a spicy, woodsy smell that reminded her of all those long treks they used to take through Delaware State Park, a scent that she associated with the happiness she had always had in his presence. What had happened to their easy comradeship? Why couldn't they just go on the way they had before?

"Did you give in to temptation yet?" he asked as he reentered the room pulling a rugby shirt down over his head. "I put your clothes in the dryer. They should be done before too long."

''Thanks. And no, I didn't give in. I wouldn't read this unless you really wanted me to.'' She tried to sound indignant, but couldn't quite pull it off. She thought honesty might be disarming so she said, ''But I'm dying to know what's in them.''

''I'll bet.'' He pulled the books out of her hands, studied them for a few seconds, and then shrugged. ''I . . . there's nothing. It's like I started to tell you that day . . . that day at the pond . . . when your mom called.'' It seemed like a lifetime ago, but it was actually less than two months.

''What? What did you start to tell me?''

''That I . . . darn it, Rebecca, it's not like you're a little kid anymore!''

''Thank goodness someone finally realized that,'' she growled dangerously.

''Oh, I realized it a long time ago. I realized it long before anyone else. That was the trouble.''

She thought they must be talking at cross purposes, but she couldn't stop herself from wanting to know what he meant. ''I don't understand.''

''It's just that my father was right.'' He tossed the books back on the floor and flopped on the far end of the couch. ''I was twenty-one years old, you were only sixteen, and I was definitely not to be trusted.''

Rebecca giggled. The sound horrified her, especially when she saw the thunderclouds on his face, but when she tried to hold it in she just giggled more. ''Oh, come on, Josh. You have always been the most trustworthy, overprotective person on the face of the earth. What was it you said in that letter? You felt like my big brother. How could your father worry, knowing you?''

"Actually, he was right to worry." He stared into the fire, ignoring her laughter.

"Oh, come on." She stopped laughing and sounded irritated. "I don't care what kind of adolescent hormonal surges you were experiencing, you never, ever put any kind of moves on me. I was just Colleen's little sister. I was a gopher for your science experiments." She blushed with the memory of her sixteenth birthday, when she had deliberately put on makeup and a dress to try proving to him that she was more than just a kid. His response had been one of exasperation, and he had gone off alone. "You didn't even think of me as a girl!"

He turned toward her now with that same look of exasperation. "Now that is just plain stupid, Rebecca. It might have been true when you were just a kid, but by the time you were sixteen, I definitely thought of you as a girl!"

His anger surprised her now, as it had when she was sixteen, but with eight years' experience she understood better. Her eyes opened wider with the pleasant shock of suddenly realizing how she might have affected him. "Do you mean that?" she asked softly.

His irritation faded and he looked embarrassed and vulnerable. "Of course I do. I really was too old for you, but you sure did look and act old enough for me. I think my dad probably saved both our hides, in spite of my protests." Restlessly he stood again, moving to the fireplace where he played with the poker for a few minutes before setting it aside and shoving his hands into his jeans pockets. "I'm still too old for you," he said without looking at her.

Rebecca watched him in amazement before her own irritation flared. "What do you mean? I thought you finally realized that I'm not a kid anymore. I've been an adult for several years now!'' She stood up and walked to stand beside him. ''Are you going to go on treating me like I'm eleven years old for the rest of my life?'' Unexpected tears filled her eyes and she raised her voice to cover them. ''I grew up as fast as I could for you, but when I finally made it, you ran away! You spent years trying to get me to be independent, and now you're trying to throw me to someone else.''

''Throw you to someone else.'' He stared at her in shock. ''What are you talking about?''

''I know all about it. You and my parents, at least my dad, conniving to make me go out on dates. I can't believe you. And making them get rid of Patty so I would have more time to do it. I don't think I'll ever forgive any of you for that!'' All the remaining chill thawed in her fury and she felt the sharp angry needles of her abandonment.

''Rebecca, I don't know what you're talking about!'' Josh felt his own temper rising quickly. What was happening to him? He used to be able to tolerate any mood Rebecca tossed at him, but these days he flared up just as quickly as she did. He yelled back, ''Stop yelling at me and tell me what you're talking about!''

''I'm talking about you wanting me to learn how to date, and Dad telling Colleen that Patty couldn't stay at the farm anymore because I hadn't been out on any dates. You didn't have any right to tell them to send Patty away!''

''I didn't do that!'' The accusation infuriated him even more. ''How stupid do you think I am? Even if I didn't like Patty so much, I would never do anything so stupid as to try to have her sent away. Why would I want to hurt you like that? Why would I want one more thing to get in the way of my being able to tell you I love you? I've put this off for nearly ten years, and I'm about to go crazy! And why would I want you to date someone else? For crying out loud, Rebecca, I've gone nuts trying to figure out how to get you to date *me!*''

She opened her mouth to shout back at him and then shut it just as quickly. Her brain worked frantically to catch up to her emotions and she opened and closed her mouth again. Her fists curled in frustration and she struggled against the urge to start throwing punches again.

Josh scowled furiously at her. She stood toe to toe with him, the firelight casting a deep glow that enhanced her flushed skin, and Josh thought she looked like a creature made of flame. He had been watching her for thirteen years, but he thought she had never looked more wild and beautiful than she did now.

He cursed inwardly for letting her make him lose his temper. He had just proven true all those things his father had warned him about. He was an intimidating monster and he was not to be trusted. With clenched teeth and an overwhelming sense of the futility of it all he turned away from her and glared instead at the burning logs.

"I'm sorry." He sighed.

"Why did you wait so long to tell me?" she asked at the same time.

"What?" They both responded at the same time and then stared at each other in a kind of confused hope. Rebecca finally stepped into the silence.

"You said that you love me."

"I do. If you don't know it by now, you must be deaf, blind, and stupid. I know you aren't any of those things, so I don't think this is really that much of a shock to you."

She looked down and shook her head. "No. I just couldn't understand why you fought so hard against it. Like it was something you couldn't help, but didn't want."

"Well, now you know."

"Yes." She felt his eyes on her but couldn't face him yet. "You didn't talk my father into sending Patty away." It wasn't a question.

"No."

"I owe you an apology for ever thinking you would have done that. I should have known better."

"Yes."

Now her eyes flew up in rebelliousness. "But you owe me an apology, too."

Josh lifted an eyebrow in question.

"You didn't trust me, either." She glowered at him as she continued. "You treated me like a weakling. From the beginning, you didn't tell me how you felt because you thought I was too young to handle it."

"You were."

"But not now. Not this time. Not for a very long time. You should have known better, too."

With a contrite smile, Josh nodded. "You're right. I'm sorry. I'll try not to let it happen again."

"Well, okay then."

"Okay then."

Silence held them again, only a foot apart but still not quite able to cross the barrier between them.

"Rebecca?"

He whispered her name and his voice and eyes

asked the question he had waited nearly half a lifetime to ask her, the question she had waited more than half a lifetime to hear. With the lightest of touches he lifted her chin until she finally raised her eyes to meet his. Every nerve in her body called to him, every corner of her spirit, and she fought against it reflexively until she realized how foolish she was being.

"Josh, I love you, too."

He pulled her into his arms, then, bringing her home. He bent close to her face, touching her lips lightly with his, still afraid of the strength of his feelings for her, still determined to be careful. With a simultaneous sigh, they tightened their arms around each other, melding with an ease that would have surprised them if they had stopped to think about it. Josh murmured her name over and over as he passed his mouth over her skin and hair. He wanted to keep her here, just holding her this closely, for as long as he could. If she pulled away from him, he feared he would never have her back again.

Rebecca floated in a state of hyper-awareness of both contentment and longing, amazed that for the first time in a long time she felt no fear. She didn't fear Joshua. His voice, his lips, and his hands expressed only tenderness and appreciation. Finally she understood that he had not left her because he didn't love her, he had left because he *did* love her. And all the time he waited for her, he continued to love her.

Josh moved his hands slowly up and down her back, trailing kisses along her neck from her ear to the collar of the robe. "My father was right," he whispered with a soft laugh. "I'm really not to be trusted."

"That makes two of us," Rebecca retorted as she placed her hands on the sides of his face and pulled him back to kiss her mouth. Her heart pounded, the blood roared in her ears, singing, ringing, ringing. "Oh, no. The phone."

"Forget the phone," Josh insisted. "The machine will get it." He nuzzled her ear, and Rebecca found it quite easy not to listen to the ringing any more.

"Hello? Hello, Josh? This is Faye. Faye Traynor . . . I'm trying to reach Bitsy, and she's not answering her phone. . . . If you see her, could you tell her that Amanda needs to talk to her this afternoon about the floral arrangements for the wedding. . . . We really need Bitsy. . . ."

Josh sighed and pulled away to reach for the phone. "I am just going to have to accept the fact that I have to share you with a dozen other people," he whispered with a laugh.

But Rebecca put her hand on his arm to stop him. She leaned over to the answering machine and turned the volume down as low as it could go. "Forget the phone, Josh," she whispered back to him. "The machine will get it."

Epilogue

Snaking its way out to one of the islands like a great feathered sea serpent, the Canadian goose hissed a warning for all to stay away from his gander and goslings. The racket startled the great blue heron standing knee-deep on the other side of the pond, and he lifted on silent wings to his own nest high in a nearby cottonwood. The tiny wood duckling, staring at the six-foot drop from its nest to the damp forest floor, ignored the other birds, thought better of the long drop, and tumbled easily back into his own comfortable nest to wait for lunch.

The adequacy of that lunch pleased Josh Mason as he finished his report on the mayfly count at the ponds. In spite of the disruption from the creation of the boardwalks and special access areas, the wetlands were thriving with plant and animal life. Already the willows were showing signs of rapid growth, their yellow-green leaves bursting out of the sides of the plain gray sticks, and the grass shooting up through the open-worked paving stones might actually require cutting at some point. The wheelchair-bound students complained with good-natured intent that they had to work too hard to get to their work.

Josh raised his eyes from his clipboard and surveyed the seven students spread out around the park planting the last of their greenhouse starts. Their final visit for this school year brought closure to Rebecca's project, but she had been unable to attend. Now the blaring of the horn on the school van shattered the pastoral scene and called the students to return to school.

"Everybody pack up and get back to the bus," called the classroom teacher.

"Okay, Ms. White." The acquiescence came quickly today.

"Thanks for helping us out, Dr. Mason," Ms. White spoke as Josh approached her. "I'm sorry Rebecca couldn't be here today. We're certainly going to miss her."

Josh nodded. "I will, too. But you know how grants are . . . never last long enough. Anyway, I guess she's ready to move on to other things."

"I expect you'll have a lot of adjusting to do yourself."

"That's the truth. I'm not sure I'm ready for all the construction out here, but I suppose the naturalist's station and those new flush toilets will come in handy for all the volunteers we'll get working here."

Cindy White raised a skeptical eyebrow. "That wasn't exactly what I meant."

Josh smiled silently and they walked toward the

special school bus. "No, I didn't think that's what you meant."

"Well, we'll be glad to have her full-time in the school system again. She's a natural teacher and a great horticultural therapist. We can use her skills in our vocational education department."

They reached the bus in time for Josh to help the driver fasten the lift door after raising the last student. Ms. White double-checked the safety locks and the bus rumbled down the new asphalt road. With only a few weeks left before summer vacation, the kids were noisy, happy, and oblivious to adult concerns about grant money, jobs, and adjusting to major changes.

Josh watched the bus out of sight and then let himself into the sharply hot truck, wishing he had rolled the windows down, surprised at the unusual May warmth. He let the fresh air blow through the truck as he took the county road up through Delaware County toward the reservoir. The old shortcut could still save a person ten minutes and he sped toward the hidden dirt road where he had first met Rebecca. A dark green Taurus blocked the turnoff, and two women and a girl dragged branches across the entrance.

"Hey! What are you doing?" he called to them, the three heads all lifting at once to notice his arrival.

"If this is May, these must be killdeer," Rebecca answered with a laugh.

"You know, if you didn't work so hard to protect these birds, they'd give up this nesting site and find one that's safer."

Colleen dropped her branch and joined her sister. "You don't know us very well, do you? We like doing things the hard way."

They watched as Patty resumed her efforts to pile

more wood in front of the flat nest. She stopped her
work and came immediately when her mother called
her.

"Say hello to Josh, Patty," Colleen urged.

"Hello, Josh," she obeyed, holding out her hand to
shake his.

"Hello, Patty, I'm very glad you're here."

"Josh and Bitsy are getting married, Mommy," she
stated quite clearly. "Josh and Bitsy are getting married, Mommy."

"We sure are, Patty, and we're glad you're here for
the wedding." Rebecca snaked her arm around Josh's
waist, and he draped his arm over her shoulder.

Josh offered to help Rebecca finish the barricade
and Colleen drove on toward the farm with her daughter. "Any problems?" he asked.

"Not at all. You could hear that she's made some
real progress with her communication, and there's a
good chance she'll do well in the public school's special program now. Colleen's going to volunteer in the
horticultural therapy program, so she'll be more
closely involved. I think they're going to be fine."

He dumped the last load of branches, pulled her
toward him, and kissed her lightly on the forehead.
"And you?"

"Well, I had to argue for our getting a turn to keep
her when Colleen and Chuck need a break. My dad
claimed that newlyweds need time alone. I finally convinced him that we truly wanted to have her with us,
but that I would happily give up the opportunity to
teach the nephews how to drive the tractor. He looked
awfully smug about it all." She savored the work-
warm smell of him and held him close. "We do need
time alone."

The plaintive cry of the male killdeer captured their attention and they watched him flutter along the side of the road in an attempt to lure them farther away from his nest. Even though they knew it was an act, they respected his performance and removed themselves back to the truck.

"Maybe fathers know more than we think they do." He laughed, admiring the killdeer's success.

"I guess we'll know for sure when it's your turn." Rebecca returned the laugh as they climbed into the truck. "Somehow, I suspect you'll be just as protective as that killdeer."

They sat quietly for a few minutes, simply enjoying the late-spring afternoon, not anxious to rush back to the hectic demands of family, both remembering the first spring they had helped protect a killdeer nest along this road.

"Thank you, Josh," Rebecca whispered. "Thank you for remembering my name. Thank you for always seeing beyond my camouflage. Thank you for being patient enough to wait for me."

"You are more than worth the wait, my love. Like the harvest at the project site. Your kids planted a huge crop of seedlings today, and I'm convinced the place is going to be beautiful. Your plan was perfect."

Rebecca sighed contentedly with the compliment and replied, "Well, you reap what you sow."

Josh leaned across the seat of the truck, pulled her close, and kissed her soundly. "In that case, Rebecca, I'd say you are going to have a bountiful harvest of love."